Not Running Away

Melissa Gijsbers

Finish This Book Press

ISBN: 978-1-7641755-5-5

For those who take brave steps, even when they don't feel brave at all

Contents

Chapter 1

⋅ ♥ ⋅ ♥ ⋅ ♥ ⋅ ♥ ⋅

'Gemma Duncan, you have officially lost your mind!' Gemma rolled her eyes at her sister's comment and continued packing her suitcase.

'I have not,' she replied.

'Yes, you have. For the first time in your life, you're a lady of leisure. You're on your own, your kids have grown up, and you're on long service leave,' her sister said. Gemma could hear the exasperation in her sister's voice. 'You're meant to be living it up, not running away to some seaside town to do some work in the lead up to Christmas.'

'Sarah,' Gemma paused her packing and turned to look at her sister. 'Long service leave isn't all it's cracked up to be. I'm bored. There are only so many cupboards you can declutter. The staff at the local op shop know me by name now, with all the trips I do there to donate unwanted items. I need a change of scenery.'

'Then go to Bali, or on a cruise, or on some other holiday. Don't take a job.'

Gemma stared at her sister.

'What about the kids?' Sarah asked.

'What about them?' Gemma went through to her ensuite to pack her toiletries. 'Joe is on year three or maybe year four of his gap year. Last I heard he was in Italy. Sammy may still be at home, but she's nearly 21 and knows how to feed herself. I'm sure she'll be fine for a few weeks.'

'I still think you've lost your mind,' Sarah said.

'Possibly,' Gemma replied. 'Either way, this is something different and new. Plus, it's way too long since I've been on my own, truly on my own.'

'You've been on your own for 20 years,' Sarah tried to argue.

'Not really, the kids have been here,' Gemma said. 'I've spent that time doing school runs, sports days, doctor's appointments, and everything else that a mum does. Even in the evenings, I couldn't go out anywhere as I had to be home for the kids.'

'What about your real job?'

'What about it?' Gemma said. 'I'm on long service leave, remember. I'm not due back at school until the end of January. This is a four-week contract, I'll be home before Christmas. Besides, this looks like a fun project.'

'Are you sure?'

'It's going through and sorting out the archives of the local Carols by Candlelight in Sapphire Bay. It's something I've always thought would be fun.'

'But you're a teacher,' Sarah said.

'I know,' replied Gemma. 'But archivist was something I was interested in doing when I was a teenager, the careers counsellor, along with mum and dad, suggested that being a history teacher would be better as there were more jobs, so I did that.'

'Fine,' Sarah said. 'I still think you've lost your mind.'

'I'll be back for Christmas,' Gemma reminded her. 'You can help Sammy decorate the tree. Besides, aren't we all going to your place on Christmas day?'

'Hmmm,' Sarah said.

'Now, have I forgotten anything,' Gemma looked at her suitcase and tried to think through everything she would need for the next month. 'I think I've got everything.'

'You're not so far away, you can always come back if you need something,' Sarah said, trying to be helpful. Gemma wasn't sure of her motives in reminding her of the distance. It was a couple of hours drive away, so she could pop back for the weekend if she needed to but really hoped that wouldn't be necessary.

'True, and I'm sure they have shops in Sapphire Bay.'

'That too.'

'Help me get the stuff to the car, I need to hit the road, I don't want to arrive when it's dark,' Gemma said. Sarah grumbled but got up to help her sister get her suitcase, backpack, laptop bag, and handbag downstairs and put them by the front door.

'Leaving already?' Sammy came out of the kitchen carrying a large hot pink, insulated mug with a straw in one hand and a half-eaten piece of toast in the other. Gemma didn't know why she needed a drink that big, but these mugs seemed to be all the rage right now.

'Yep, I was about to find you to say goodbye,' Gemma replied.

'Well, have fun,' Sammy said, already heading for the stairs.

'What, no hug?' Gemma said, trying to act like she was hurt when she really wasn't surprised. It had been many years since she'd been a priority in her children's lives. Sammy came back down the stairs and gave her mum a quick kiss on the cheek.

'Bye, mum,' she said. 'Bye Aunty Sarah.' Sammy headed back upstairs without a backwards glance at her mother or aunt. Gemma turned to her sister.

'See, the kids will be fine,' she said. She picked up her bags and headed to the car.

***

Driving down the highway, Gemma slipped a CD that she had discovered while she was decluttering into the CD player. At the top of one of the cupboards in her house was a box of CDs that she had forgotten about. This was her music, not Joe's or Sammy's or her ex-husbands, this was the music she enjoyed. It had been years since she'd listened to it.

The sound filled the car, and she turned up the volume. As she drove, she sang along with music that took her straight back to her teenage years. Her mind wandered back to thoughts of lying on her bed with Sarah listening to this same CD and ignoring their parents telling them to turn down the volume. Fighting with her sister who always wanted to borrow her stuff. Dreaming of travelling the world and exploring historic sights, maybe even being part of an archaeological dig in Egypt. Dreaming of falling in love with a rock star. All the usual teenage things.

A song came on that transported her to year 12 formal and thoughts turned to the roads not travelled. What if she had married Scott, the boy she went to the formal with instead of marrying Harry when she was at university. Would she have had Joe and Sammy? Would she still be a teacher? It was a career she loved, but was there something else for her?

She knew she'd been feeling restless; that was one of the reasons she'd applied for the contract with the Sapphire Bay carols. She didn't yet know what she wanted, only that she hoped this break would help her find some clarity.

The sun was starting to set as Gemma pulled into the Sapphire Bay Beachside Apartments. She wasn't usually a fan of daylight savings but today she was grateful as it meant she wasn't arriving somewhere new in the dark.

The complex was a collection of six townhouses, each with a carport on the ground floor and a balcony overlooking the beach. They were cream and had clearly been there for decades, the paint overdue for an update. A few sad-looking palm trees dotted the front of the property. Most of the units looked unoccupied, except for unit 6 at the far end as there was a car in the carport. Even though the townhouses looked old, they were also welcoming and Gemma thought this looked as good a place as any to stay for four weeks. An added bonus was it was a short walk to the library where she would be working.

Gemma paused and looked at her phone for the instructions on how to get inside. She was in unit 2 and there was a lockbox near the front door with the keys. She started the car again and pulled into the carport for unit 2.

She got out of the car, took her luggage and went to the front door. The lockbox was where the email told her it would be. She found the keys and let herself in. The entryway was small, but clean, with a tiled floor and some prints of beach scenes on the walls. From the description she'd been given, she knew there was one bedroom and a bathroom that doubled as a laundry on the ground floor, but she wasn't interested in that, instead going straight to the stairs and pulling her luggage behind her.

At the top of the stairs was an open plan area with a kitchen and living room at the front of the house and two bedrooms behind her. The front of the house was covered with blackout curtains. The only light came from a skylight above the kitchen. Instead of reaching for the light switch, Gemma left her luggage in the middle of the room and pushed open the curtains. She stepped out through the glass doors and onto the balcony and gasped.

The view was nothing short of spectacular. The sun was nearly set over the sea, causing shadows and glints of light on the water. It was mesmerising. She walked towards the railing of the balcony almost as if in a trance and she stood there, taking in every detail of the view in front of her.

Sapphire Bay is well named, she thought as she took it all in.

She didn't move until the sun dipped below the horizon, feeling a sense of peace fall on her. For the first time since she applied for the job, she didn't feel like she was running away from anything, despite her words to her sister. It felt like she had arrived somewhere special and was exactly where she needed to be.

She turned and went back into the apartment to turn a light on. She smiled seeing a welcome basket on the counter with a note explaining there was cheese and wine from local producers in the fridge and to enjoy them with the crackers and olives in the basket. The basket also had tea and coffee, and there was milk in the fridge as well.

Gemma poured herself a glass of wine, grateful for this small gift, and went back out to the balcony to look at the water in the moonlight. This was meant to be a short job in a seaside town, and even though she had only just arrived, it already felt as though this was the beginning of something.

Chapter 2

'Happy Monday, Adam.' Adam stopped at the library counter as he heard the cheerful welcome and his name. He'd decided on a short cut through the library to his office on the first floor of the council building. Margaret, one of the librarians, stood there wearing a t-shirt that said 'Seasons Readings' with piles of books and Christmas trees on it.

'Morning, Margaret,' he replied. 'It's mid-November, isn't it a little early for the Christmas t-shirts?'

'Never too early,' Margaret replied with a grin. 'Besides, if I don't start now, I won't get through them all.' Adam smiled, he believed her and knew her collection grew every year with the office kris kringle. 'Isn't the carols research project starting today?'

'It is,' Adam said. 'I can't wait.'

'A bit nervous?' Adam threw her a confused look. 'You always go paddleboarding in the morning if you're nervous.'

'How did you…' he began. Margaret laughed.

'Your hair is still wet,' she said. 'And I've known you since you were a small boy.' Adam laughed. Margaret was about 15 years older than he was, and she had babysat him when she was in high school, but the way she talked made it sound like she was his grandmother.

'Right,' Adam replied. 'I do go paddleboarding on other days too.' Margaret raised her eyebrows. 'Fine, I'm nervous about this. I'm grateful the committee was able to get a grant for this work, but sorting the archives is not going to convince the council to change.'

'They should have included it...' Margaret said.

'We've talked about this before,' Adam said. 'I'm sure it was an oversight; there's no one to blame.'

'Yeah, right,' Margaret said. 'We can't lose the space on the foreshore.'

'Exactly,' Adam said. 'That's why we are doing this project. Maybe she will dig up something that will help, but I know that's not part of the brief.'

'What do you know about this researcher?'

'Her name is Gemma Duncan. She's from the city, a history teacher on long service leave,' Adam said, reciting the information that had been passed on to him by Julie Nolan, the head of the Carols by Candlelight committee.

'And why are you meeting her and not Julie?'

'Because I work here,' Adam said. 'I may be upstairs in the accounting office, but I'm on site. Julie works in the gift shop at the other end of town and things are getting busy in the lead up to Christmas.'

'Makes sense, what time is she getting here?'

'At eleven,' Adam said, checking his watch. 'That doesn't leave me much time to get some work done before she gets here. Could you buzz me if I'm late coming down, I'm hoping to be back here before she arrives?'

'Of course,' Margaret said with a twinkle in her eye. 'You owe me Adam Cooper.'

'Add it to the list,' Adam said. 'See you around eleven.'

He headed upstairs to his office. He hadn't been part of the recruitment process for the research assistant position, and he hoped the committee had chosen well. He had seen other towns where events such as the Carols by Candlelight had had to move away from the places that had made them special and they had fizzled out. He couldn't let that happen in Sapphire Bay.

The computer on his desk came to life and he tried to focus on processing invoices from suppliers. A photo on his desk caught his eye. It was an old one, and one of his favourites. He was about ten, part of the school choir, with both his parents on stage: his mum conducting, his dad in the band, and him just visible at the side. It had been the only time the whole family had been on stage together, and he kept it as a reminder of what the Carols could mean: a community coming together, families taking part, everyone having a role. He stared at it for a moment and wished his dad was still with them and made a mental note to call his mum and see how she was doing.

Adam recognised that he simply wasn't going to be focusing on the invoices, so he got up and went to the kitchenette at the end of the floor to get some coffee, more to work off nervous energy than actually needing a the caffeine. He knew the council had spent a long time developing the plans for the foreshore development, and they had done so without as much community consultation as anyone expected. They had engaged a fancy city firm and had forgotten the community aspect of their town, instead focusing on commerce.

It's not just the carols, he thought as he waited for the coffee machine to do its thing. *It's also the community market, and so much more.* He knew many events had stopped in 2020 due to the lockdowns and hadn't started up again, and he had hoped that a redeveloped community space would be the catalyst for those events returning.

He headed back to his desk and started to watch the clock for 10:55am, really hoping that Gemma Duncan could perform some sort of Christmas miracle.

Chapter 3

Gemma reluctantly got out of bed. She was wide awake earlier than she'd wanted to, hoping for a bit of a lie in after her long drive the night before. She didn't have to be at the library to get things started until 11am, she had plenty of time.

She decided to take her laptop and walk down the street and treat herself to breakfast before her meeting rather than hanging about in the apartment. She figured this was a tourist town so there was sure to be somewhere with good coffee.

As she walked, she stopped to look out over the bay. It was a magical place with sunlight glinting off the water. There were paddleboarders enjoying the morning calm, and Gemma stopped to watch for a while. She wished she had her camera with her, not the one on her phone, but the one she had been given as a teenager when she went through a period where photography was her passion. It had years since she had packed it away and was surprised her to think about it now.

I must see if it's still at Mum and Dad's, she thought, knowing it wasn't at her house.

As she mused, she saw a man emerge from the water on to the beach. He shook his head and water flew from his hair. He was wearing a wetsuit and carried a paddleboard under one arm. She smiled to herself with a fleeting thought that the view here was spectacular. She giggled, she was a 49 year-old single mother of two grown children, not a 20 something looking for a man, but the thought was fun.

Her stomach rumbled as she roused herself to go and find a café for breakfast and possibly start doing some research about the carols before heading to the library.

As she walked, she noticed signs being installed advertising the carols for the week before Christmas.

'That's good,' she thought, thinking that it should have a good turnout by the community, and getting excited at the thought of what treasures may lie in the archive boxes that she was going to be sorting out.

***

It didn't seem long before the alarm on Gemma's phone rang and it was time to head to the library to meet her contact from the carols committee and find out more about what she needed to do.

She had found a café across the road from the library with some tables out front so she could enjoy her latte and blueberry pancakes while doing some basic research about the Sapphire Bay Carols by Candlelight. As far as she could tell, they started at some point in the 1950s or maybe early 1960s, but she hadn't been able to find out the exact year. It had run every year since, even during 2020 and 2021 when crowd limits had meant they introduced livestreaming. The livestreamed carols had been very popular, and videos were still on the Internet and they had thousands of views. By her calculations, the carols were coming up to 70 or 75, maybe even 80 years. She made a note to work it out.

It was with some reluctance that she closed her laptop. She was enjoying this trip down the rabbit hole of research, then she remembered that her job was sorting out the archive boxes, and she figured that would be even more fun.

She paid for her breakfast and nearly ran across the road to the council buildings. She was early, as usual, but had time to go to the bathroom and make sure she didn't have any spots of blueberry on her face or her top. When she was happy that everything looked as it should, even though her hair was a little windswept from the walk from the apartment and running from the café, she went to the main counter of the library.

'How can I help you?' Gemma was greeted at the counter by an older woman wearing a Christmas t-shirt.

'Hi, I'm Gemma Duncan, I'm meant to be meeting...' Gemma paused and looked at her phone, worried she would get the name wrong. 'Adam Cooper.'

'Ahhh, you must be Gemma, I'm Margaret,' the woman held out her hand to Gemma. 'Adam shouldn't be too far away.'

'Nice to meet you,' said Gemma, starting to feel a bit overwhelmed at this welcome. Her eyes fell to Margaret's t-shirt.

'It's never too early for some Christmas cheer,' Margaret said. Gemma looked away almost guiltily. 'I know it's only November, but it hasn't been the easiest of years.' Gemma gave a tight smile. Margaret wasn't wrong about the year, that feeling of being all at sea had been with her all year, but a Christmas t-shirt in November?

Gemma was saved from further small talk by the arrival of a tall man who looked around her age. He was cleanly shaven with a head of salt and pepper hair that made him look quite dashing. Gemma thought he looked familiar, but she couldn't quite place him.

'Hi, I'm Adam, you must be Gemma,' he greeted her with a smile and held out his hand to shake.

'Um, yes,' she smiled back and took his hand. It was warm and strong.

'Great to have you here, come on through and I'll show you what needs to be done.' He turned around and started walking through the library, Gemma was grateful there wasn't more small talk and she followed. As they went through, she was impressed with the library facilities. It was in an older building, yet it looked as though the insides had been renovated recently and it looked modern and inviting with banks of computers, shelves full of books, places for people to sit, and even a space for locals to record podcasts.

Adam stopped at a door and Gemma nearly bumped into him; she was too busy looking around. He used a swipe card to enter a back room.

'Here you go,' he announced as they entered. 'This will be your home for the next few weeks.'

Gemma looked around the room and sneezed. This part of the building obviously hadn't been part of the renovations. The carpet looked straight out of the 1970s and the walls had spots where paint was peeling. There were some windows high up on one of the walls, and under them were rows of metal shelves with old archive boxes, some were labelled, some weren't, and they were in various stages of disrepair. These shelves were on two of the walls and there were some trestle tables against another with an old office chair for her to sit on. As well as the boxes, there were stacks of photo albums and VHS tapes, and other bits and pieces that Gemma couldn't quite identify.

'Wow, that looks like a lot...' Gemma said.

'It hasn't been a priority for anyone to organise all of this or digitise it, so it didn't happen. When the library was renovated, anything that looked like it was part of the Carols by Candlelight history and should be kept was shoved in here, it may not be purely carol related, though.' Adam looked around the room and shook his head. Then Gemma realised.

'You were on the beach this morning, with your paddle board,' she blurted, then blushed in a way she hadn't since she was a teenager. He stared at her. 'I'm sorry, I was walking along the beach this morning and watching the paddle boarders. When I met you just now, I thought you looked familiar,' her words stumbled over themselves. 'I'm sorry, I...'

'It's alright,' he chuckled. 'Have you ever been paddleboarding?' Gemma shook her head; glad this moment hadn't turned into something awkward. 'Maybe one day I can take you out?' he suggested.

'Sounds good,' Gemma replied vaguely. She got the feeling this was a genuine offer, one to help her enjoy her time here rather than a romantic suggestion.

'Right, let's get on to this,' he said, changing the subject. 'As the committee explained to you, all of this needs to be organised so we know what we've got.' Gemma nodded. 'Maybe this can help convince the council to keep it...' his voice trailed off. 'Let me show you around and get you a swipe card.'

Gemma followed Adam out of the room and he took her to the security desk for a card and showed her where to make coffee. She had the feeling there was more to this job than simply sorting the archives and, as she settled down to get started, she hoped she would have the opportunity to ask him.

Chapter 4

Adam left Gemma to start organising the storeroom while he went to get on with his other work. She managed to open the windows in the hope that it would reduce some of the stuffiness in the room and got to work.

She surveyed the mess and figured the place to start was to sort things by decade and could go from there. Thankfully the room was fairly large and she could spread out, though there was a lot of junk to go through. As she went, she used a notebook to make notes of anything particularly interesting and thought that she should ask for some sticky notes to help with the process.

'Hey,' Adam entered the room, startling Gemma. She was going through a box that contained random flyers and newspaper clippings, some were from the carols and some were from other events held at the foreshore. For now, she had decided to sort them by decade too, more for her own interest.

'Hey, yourself,' Gemma said.

'It's after 1pm, want to get some lunch?' Gemma hadn't noticed the time fly by and, when her tummy rumbled, she realised she hadn't eaten since the pancakes at breakfast.

'Sounds good,' she stretched her arms above her head.

'It's on me, come on, we'll head to my favourite eatery,' Adam said. Gemma sneezed from the dust, the open windows hadn't done their job very well, and followed him out. She made a mental note to ask about a vacuum cleaner. He locked the door to the room behind him and Gemma stopped at the bathroom to wash her hands before joining him at the door to the library.

'I know you've only just started,' Adam began as they walked up the street together. 'But have you found anything interesting?'

'Other than the place being a mess?' Gemma joked. 'I did find a box of flyers, it looks like the foreshore has been a hub of community activities for decades, not just the carols, is that what you mean by interesting?'

'It's a start,' Adam said. Gemma couldn't quite read his tone.

'Did you have anything in mind?'

'It's a great start, I know there's a monthly market in the Summer months,' Adam said.

'There's been so much more than that,' Gemma said, surprising herself with how strongly she felt about it. 'It looks like there's been everything from music festivals to surfing competitions going back, I think the earliest I've seen so far was the early '70s, but there could be more.'

'I didn't know we had ever had a music festival,' said Adam. 'I've lived here most of my life.'

'As far as I can tell, and this is just from flyers at this stage, it was every couple of years in the 70s and 80s, they had some big names too. It's a pity how many events come and go over the years,' Gemma said almost wistfully, remembering events she had enjoyed as a child.

'They must have stopped when I was small, I don't remember them,' said Adam.

'Well, here we are,' Adam said, stopping at a food truck that was set up outside a pet shop. 'They have the best burgers here.'

They ordered and sat down at a makeshift table to eat their lunch.

'Tell me, Adam,' Gemma said after they had been silent for a while. 'Tell me about the carols, they seem important to you. I mean to you, not just the town.' She tried to make it sound light and really hoped she didn't come across as prying.

'I grew up here,' he said. 'When I was at school, the primary school choir would perform each year. In high school, there were other opportunities to get involved. It showed us teens that we were part of the community, at least at Christmas. My whole family was involved too. My mum occasionally conducted the choir, my dad in the band, and other years we were part of the audience. Everyone would come out and have fun that night.'

As he shared his memories, Gemma saw his face light up. He told her about the year the stage collapsed, thankfully with no injuries, the performers just moved to one side and kept going. He told her about the old couple who hosted it during the 1990s, they had retired to Sapphire Bay after decades in show business, and came, year after year, to host the event. There was a story about a young man Adam had gone to school with who learned stage craft by volunteering with the event and that was what kept him out of trouble, it gave him a purpose. He had been working in the industry for years now, working with some of the largest stage productions around Australia and overseas.

The more Adam shared with her, the more she saw the carols were more than a concert, more than the performers. It was the heart of the community.

'Given all of this,' Gemma said when Adam seemed to come to an end. 'What did you mean when you mentioned convincing the council to keep it?' Adam stared at Gemma for a moment. He took a deep breath before replying.

'The council have decided to redevelop the foreshore precinct,' Adam said. 'They got some bigwigs from the city to come and do the redesign, but with a focus on commerce rather than community. There isn't any space for large community events in their plans.'

'What does that mean?' she asked.

'They have planned a jetty and space for cafés and picnic tables, and that's about it,' Adam said. He got out his phone, typed for a moment and turned it to show her. 'See?'

Gemma looked at the plans. They certainly looked fancy with walkways and designer picnic tables dotted along the way. There were spaces for shops and cafés. She could see what Adam meant by there being no space for large events.

'There's no playground either!' she exclaimed. 'Do you think this was deliberate?' she asked. Adam shook his head.

'I don't think so. I think those who were planning this didn't think about it. From what I've seen they're used to designing spaces in the city rather than regional communities,' he said. 'My theory is the council simply deprioritised it, having event space wasn't in the tender brief. We've been told the carols could be held somewhere else, but it will lose the magic of having the bay behind it, not to mention most of the ovals aren't big enough for an event like this, and not enough parking.'

Gemma nodded. She had been in Sapphire Bay less than 24 hours and had already seen how magical that view was. She could only imagine what an impact it would have on an event like the carols.

'I'm hoping that you may find something as you sort through the archives, something that can convince the council that they need to have event space in their plans,' Adam said.

'I see,' said Gemma, realising she truly did. 'I'll be sure to keep that in mind as I go through things.'

Adam looked at her and grinned, his eyes sparkling with excitement.

'I'm glad you understand,' he said. Gemma smiled back at him. She collected her lunch rubbish and stood up.

'I do,' she said. 'So, I'd better get back to it.'

As they walked back, she felt a ripple of excitement run through her. The idea that this was now a treasure hunt made things more interesting and she couldn't wait to see what may be in the storeroom.

Chapter 5

Friday night came around and Gemma was looking forward to the weekend. She had no plans, other than to try out a couple more cafés, walk along the beach, and generally explore Sapphire Bay. She had picked up some tourist brochures at the library but wanted a quiet weekend. Her mind was still buzzing with the stories and scraps of history she'd been uncovering in the archive boxes.

She had bought some microwave meals so she wouldn't have to cook, and took one of them, a glass of wine, and a book on to the balcony to enjoy the evening sun and unwind after a busy week.

Her phone rang as she was finishing her meal. She was tempted to ignore it and stay wrapped in the peace of the evening but saw her sister's name on the screen.

'Hey, sis,' Gemma said.

'Hey yourself,' said Sarah. 'You're still alive, then.' Gemma laughed.

'Yep, still alive,' Gemma confirmed. 'You should see the view from this balcony.'

'I have seen the photos you sent through. It looks wonderful.'

'It is, I'm on the balcony now,' Gemma said. She stood up and went to lean against the railing. 'The sun is starting to go down; the light is dancing on the water...'

'And paddleboarders?' Sarah teased.

'Yep, there are some there too, I think,' Gemma said. 'They're a bit further down the beach, though.' Gemma had forgotten that she'd sent Sarah a text after she'd seen Adam on the beach on Monday morning. Adam had offered to take her one day, Gemma wasn't sure how she felt about that.

'How's the job going?' Sarah asked.

'It's amazing!' Gemma enthused. 'There is so much amazing information that I'm sorting, plus VHS tapes! I've asked Adam to see if he can find a player so we can see what's on them.'

'Adam, huh?' Sarah said. Gemma noted the teasing in her voice.

'Adam, my colleague,' Gemma said. 'He's technically my supervisor.' Gemma knew that Julie, the president of the committee, was her boss, but she'd only met her once, in passing. Adam was the one she was working closest with.

'Hmmm,' Sarah said. Gemma got the feeling her sister wasn't believing her. 'Just colleague?'

'Yes!'

'Have you been stuck in the library or have you got out a bit?' Sarah asked after a moment's silence.

'Mostly at the library,' replied Gemma. 'I have gone out for lunch with Margaret and Adam a few times.'

'Adam, huh?' Gemma knew her sister hadn't let it go.

'Honestly, Sarah, he's basically my boss.'

'Methinks thou doth protest too much,' Sarah said sweetly. Gemma wished this was a video call so she could poke her tongue out at her. 'But he's not really your boss, is he.'

'He is, kind of,' Gemma said. 'Either way, we work together, that's it. He's a nice guy.'

'You deserve a nice guy,' Sarah said. 'It's been too long.'

'Sarah, I came here for work, for a change of scenery, not for anything else,' Gemma said, getting annoyed. 'Hang on, weren't you against me coming here, saying I had lost my mind?' Sarah didn't reply. 'Anyway, the view here is amazing. There's a spare room if you want to come down and escape your kids for a night or two.'

'Tempting, but all the Christmas activities are starting, we have the footy awards night this weekend.'

'In November?'

'Yep, late this year. Have you heard from Sammy?

'Not since I got a text when she couldn't find the cheese grater, then send a message saying to not worry she was going to buy pre-grated cheese,' Gemma laughed. 'I'm sure no news is good news.'

The sisters spoke for a bit longer, Gemma shared some of the things she had discovered during her sorting out, Sarah shared some of the things she had been doing at work and with her kids.

When they ended the call, Gemma felt a pang that talking on the phone wasn't quite the same as face to face, then she looked up at the sun setting over the bay and felt that feeling of calm come over her again. She couldn't shake the teasing about Adam. He was a nice guy, a colleague. She could see them becoming good friends. She had been on her own for a long time, spending all her energy on raising her kids. Was it now time for some romance?

She shook her head. No, romance was not what she was after, besides, she was only here for another three weeks, she didn't want to start something that would go nowhere.

She turned and went inside to put the kettle on and settle down in front of a movie with a cup of tea.

Chapter 6

'Cooper!' Adam heard his mate, Richie, call as he entered the Sapphire Bay Arms, their local pub, on Friday evening.

'Richie,' Adam greeted him with a fist bump.

'We missed you on Tuesday night,' Scotty said.

'I had another offer,' said Adam, neglecting to mention the fact he had taken Gemma out for fish and chips on the beach instead of joining his mates for their weekly pub trivia night. He had told himself he was being welcoming, and that's all it was, but found he really liked her company.

'We needed your superior knowledge of daggy Christmas music,' Richie laughed.

'It's November,' Adam said. 'Surely it's a bit early for Christmas questions in trivia.'

'Margaret set them,' replied Scotty. 'Thanks mate.' He added as Benji came over with a tray of beers.

'Saw ya on the beach Tuesday night,' Benji said. 'Who were you with that was more interesting than trivia?'

'Gemma Duncan,' Adam said. 'She's here to help with the carols archives.'

'You should have brought her to trivia,' said Benji.

'Maybe another time,' said Adam.

'What does she do when she's not sorting through junk?' asked Richie.

'She's a history teacher.'

'Then you should have brought her to trivia,' said Benji. 'We did pretty badly last week.' He shook his head and Adam laughed.

'We do badly most weeks,' he laughed. The four of them had been friends since Adam had returned to Sapphire Bay after he had left for university and been away for a number of years, returning after his dad died, and to nurse a broken heart.

'True, but that's half the fun,' Scotty raised his beer glass, and they toasted their uselessness at trivia.

'But seriously,' Richie said. 'Tell us more about Gemma.' Adam rolled his eyes.

'What's to tell?' said Adam. 'She's here for a few weeks sorting out the archives for the carols.'

'Still hoping to save it?' asked Benji.

'Yep,' Adam said. 'I thought you would have been more for it as your wife sells her handmade jewellery at the foreshore markets.'

'I just figure it's a lost cause,' said Benji. 'This council never listens.'

'I'm hoping for a Christmas miracle.'

'You must really like this Gemma,' said Benji. Adam rolled his eyes.

'Anyone could have got the gig,' Adam said. As he said it, an image of Gemma went through his mind, she had a beautiful smile. He shook his head. She would be gone in a few weeks, it didn't matter.

'Promise you'll bring her to trivia on Tuesday night,' Richie was saying. 'Ireland, Linda and Amanda can come too. Maybe we could get in the top 10...'

'Of 12 teams!' Scotty laughed. Adam was glad the conversation moved on.

As he walked home, he looked out over the bay. It had been quite a few years since his wife had left him, running off with her yoga instructor. At the time he felt like he was a walking cliché, using his father dying as the official excuse to come back to Sapphire Bay. He and his mum had spent some months healing from their heartbreaks. There hadn't been anyone else in his life since then. He hadn't let there be. All week, he had been finding excuses to go to the storeroom at the back of the library to see Gemma.

He shook his head and continued walking home, trying to push thoughts of Gemma out of his head. He wouldn't see her again until Monday, and somehow he felt a bit emptier with the thought he wouldn't see her for two whole days.

Chapter 7

The next day, Gemma wandered along the beach heading towards the Foreshore complex. Margaret had been talking about the foreshore market that was on that afternoon and Gemma thought it was a great opportunity to do some Christmas shopping as well as see the place Adam had been talking about.

'Twilight markets,' she had told her sister on the phone the night before. 'That's something missing in the city. So many markets are on too early.' Sarah had agreed that a market starting at 4pm was much more civilized and had asked Gemma to pick up some gin for her husband's Christmas present, if there was some on sale.

It was only just past 4pm when she arrived at the market site and joined the people going through the stalls. For a market that had only just opened, there were quite a few people there.

Gemma was impressed at the range of products on sale, from baby clothes and toys to pet products to art and prints to homemade jams and sauces. She stopped by the stand of a local author and purchased books for her niece and nephew, hoping they still read books. Getting them signed by the author made them extra special.

She found a couple of different types of gin and took photos to send to Sarah so she could choose. She stopped by a stand that sold handmade jewellery.

'These are gorgeous,' she said, holding up some earrings that looked like tacos with cute black eyes.

'They are fun, aren't they,' the stallholder said. 'I make all of these when the kids are in bed.'

'You are so creative,' Gemma said. She knew Sammy would love the earrings. 'Do you have an online shop? My daughter will go crazy for these, so will her friends.'

'Thanks, my card is in the bag,' the woman said as she processed Gemma's payment.

'This seems like such an amazing market,' Gemma said.

'It's pretty special,' the woman said. 'The majority of the traders are from around here; the organisers have worked hard to promote local creators.'

'That's wonderful,' Gemma said and slipped the bag with the earrings in her backpack.

'I hope I'll see you again,' the woman said with a smile. 'The next market is in January.'

'Nothing in December?' The woman shook her head.

'We make way for the Carols by Candlelight. It's the event of the year.' The woman handed her a flyer. Gemma had noticed most of the stallholders had flyers or posters promoting the event on their stands.

'Thanks,' Gemma smiled and continued browsing the stalls.

By the time she got home, after eating some delicious sushi from a food truck, she was tired, her bag was full of Christmas presents, and she'd spoiled herself with a few goodies, including going back to the stall she had bought the taco earrings and bought a necklace with a polymer clay daisy pendant.

As she made herself a hot chocolate before getting ready for bed, she thought and couldn't remember when she'd enjoyed a market as much.

The stallholders were all friendly, there was a wonderful variety of products, and the community feel was strong. She thought back to Adam's comments about the foreshore redevelopment.

'It would be sad to lose that space,' she said to herself. 'And I haven't been to the Carols by Candlelight yet!' She was determined to find something in all the boxes of archive material, there had to be something to help them convince the council to change their plans.

Chapter 8

On Monday afternoon, Gemma was sitting on the floor of the storeroom surrounded by papers. She had spent the morning vacuuming the room in the hope it would reduce the time she spent sneezing before tackling some of the unlabeled boxes.

She had newspaper clippings, photographs, files of budgets, programs, and agreements with suppliers. There were scripts and tech specifications, along with lists of volunteers and minutes of committee meetings. She was excited by this goldmine of information and was having a lot of fun organising it all by decade, along with taking notes of anything that may be significant.

'You look like you're having fun,' Adam made her jump. She was engrossed in reading a script from 1963.

'You need a bell or something around your neck,' she teased. 'And yes, I am having fun.'

'Did you notice it's nearly 6pm,' he said. 'The library is closing soon.'

Gemma looked at the clock on the wall, it said 3.48.

'I think that clock has stopped,' she commented. Adam laughed.

'That one stopped more than a couple of hours ago,' he said. 'I think it's time to finish for the night.' Gemma stretched her arms over her head. Her back was sore from sitting on the floor, but she hadn't noticed until now. 'Need a hand to get up?' he offered her a hand.

'Thanks,' she took it gratefully and he helped pull her up. She stretched again to get some of the kinks out of her back. 'Sometimes I forget I'm not 16 anymore.'

'Me too,' Adam laughed with her. 'Dinner?'

'Sounds good,' Gemma said. 'But this time, I pay. You've paid the last couple of times we've eaten together.'

Adam opened his mouth as if to protest but closed it again.

'Done,' he said. 'You can update me on your progress too.'

She waved her hand to show the papers on the floor and the neat piles on the tables.

'This is pretty much it,' she said. 'As far as I can tell, the carols started in 1956, so next year would be 70 years since the event started, always on the foreshore. Even during the pandemic restrictions in 2020 and 2021, the livestream was hosted there. I watched some of the videos over the weekend, they were really good.'

'I remember,' he said. 'It was a challenge behind the scenes, especially keeping the audience numbers to the limits, but it still had a community feel.'

Gemma smiled. She grabbed her handbag and got ready to follow him out of the room.

'Where to for dinner? I may be paying, but I don't really know where to go.'

Adam grinned. 'Do you like spicy food?'

***

Over some of the most amazing curry Gemma had ever eaten, though she had asked for it not be too spicy, she took Adam through some of her notes.

'You know the singer, Abigail Freedman,' she began. Abigail Freedman had been on Australia's Got Talent as a teenager in the early 2000s, while she didn't win, she had been able to rise to stardom and was constantly in the charts with albums, had stared in a movie and was a regular guest on television shows.

'I do,' Adam said.

'She had her first solo performance at the Sapphire Bay Carols!' Gemma said. 'She was eight and sang the first verse of *Away in a Manger.*'

'That's fantastic,' Adam said. 'How did I not know that?'

'From what I can tell, her family moved out of the area before she started high school,' Gemma replied. She had spent way too long doing Internet searches for this one.

'Anything else?' Adam asked. Gemma had already filled him in on some of the other things she had found out.

'That couple you told me about, Alf and Joan Trevors, they hosted the carols during the 1990s,' Gemma said. Adam nodded. 'Did you know that Alf proposed to Joan back in 1961, at the Sapphire Bay Carols by Candlelight?'

'Were they on stage?' Adam asked. Gemma shook her head.

'Not that year,' Gemma said. 'They were in Sapphire Bay on holiday, and they were in the audience. I saw an interview on one of the daytime talk shows where Alf shared that story.' Gemma grinned. She had spent ages watching clips over the weekend.

'That's pretty cool,' Adam said.

'I've noticed something,' Gemma said. 'The carols event isn't about one big thing, one big moment. There's nothing groundbreaking about it at all. It's all the little stories, the way the event has touched the lives of those involved, whether they were on stage, backstage, or in the audience. This is an important event, and we need to get that across to the council so they can rethink their plans. Somehow, I think the council will understand if they can see the people behind it.'

'I hope it's not too late,' Adam said.

'Have the final plans been signed off yet?' Gemma asked.

'I don't think so.'

'Then, it's not too late,' Gemma said. 'We just need to convince them.'

'Something tells me you have an idea on how to do this,' said Adam. 'You must think we're so disorganised, leaving it so late.'

'Not at all,' Gemma said. 'Life can get busy, and sometimes it takes a fresh set of eyes. I don't have a plan yet, but an idea is forming.'

Gemma sipped her water and looked out the window at the twinkling streetlights. There was something about this town that made her feel she could make a difference.

Chapter 9

·ᵥ·♥·♥·♥·ᵥ·

'How's it going?' Adam popped his head around the door to the room Gemma worked in with two mugs of coffee in his hands. It was Wednesday afternoon and he hadn't seen Gemma since their dinner on Monday night. He had been surprised to notice that he was missing her. 'Coffee?'

'Mmm, thank you,' Gemma said, getting up from her chair. She took a sip. 'I was ready for a break, and things are going well.'

'Any ideas for the council?' he asked.

'I think so,' Gemma said. She indicated a rough display that she had put up on one wall. There was some blue builders tape in horizontal lines and she had marked space on it in decades. In between were sticky notes, photographs, and other documents showing highlights from nearly 70 years of the Carols by Candlelight event. 'This is a rough timeline of the event.'

Adam stood back and admired her work. The sticky notes were a variety of colours, and each had a note on them. He saw piles of notes that hadn't been added to the wall yet.

'I assume those colours aren't random,' he said.

'They're not,' Gemma confirmed. 'Yellow is general stuff, mostly things that go back in the folders, newspaper clippings, that sort of thing. Blue is performers, anything significant that I've found. Green is backstage, including things like the year the stage collapsed. Pink is audience stories, mostly from newspaper clippings or things I found online. And the other colours are for anything else. They're random as there were quite a few random colours in the box of sticky notes.' Gemma finished with a laugh. 'We can compile these stories, or some of them at least, and present them to the council at the next meeting. Then, maybe, compile them in a book or something next year to celebrate the 70th anniversary celebration next year.'

'If there is one,' Adam said flatly, though he was feeling a stirring of hope deep inside that they may be able to convince the council.

'Think positive, of course there will be,' Gemma said. Adam admired her optimism. 'When is the next council meeting?'

'Monday week,' he said. The date was seared in his head, this was the day the council was meant to announce their decision about who got the contract for the redevelopment, however, Adam knew the council wasn't always as organised as they seemed.

'Hmm, that gives us...' Gemma started counting on her fingers. 'About 10 days to make this happen. We can do it.'

Adam smiled and reached for his phone and started typing.

'What are you doing?' she asked.

'Making sure we get on the agenda,' he said. 'We can't do a presentation if we're not there.' He looked up and smiled at her. She smiled back. He felt a little shiver of excitement; things were looking up. He went back to the message he was typing. Angela was the person in charge of the agenda, and she had been his mother's best friend. He was hoping he was catching her in a good mood. He put his phone back in his pocket. 'While we're waiting for a reply, where do we start?'

Gemma leaned against the table and explained to Adam what she had in mind.

'I'm not sure how many people will get back to us,' she was saying. 'But there's no harm in reaching out to them. It's not quite archiving all of this,' she waved her hand around the room.

'It's part of it,' Adam said. 'You really have found treasure here.'

By the time Adam had left the room to go back to his desk, the mugs of coffee were cold, Angela had got back to them to let them know they would be on the agenda, and he knew this project was in good hands. He was also excited by the thought of meeting up with Gemma that night at her apartment to go through the idea of the presentation in more detail. He couldn't work out if it was just about the presentation or if it was being able to spend more time with Gemma. It had been a long time since he'd felt this way.

He got to his desk and tried to push thoughts of Gemma and the carols out of his head so he could focus for the last couple of hours of his work day.

Chapter 10

The sound of the doorbell dragged Gemma out of a deep, much-needed sleep. It had been a busy few days and she had been looking forward to a Saturday morning sleep in. The doorbell sounded again, along with some knocking on the door. She leaned over and looked at her phone; it was just before 8am.

Gemma grumbled and rolled out of bed. She put on her dressing gown and headed downstairs to see who was disturbing her sleep. She opened the door to the face of Adam. He was standing there bright-eyed dressed for the beach.

'What on earth?' she said, not sure if him on her doorstep was a good or bad thing.

'You forgot, didn't you,' he said. She saw the disappointment on his face.

'Forgot what?' She said. Then remembered. 'Oh, paddleboarding!' It had completely slipped her mind. 'Umm...'

'How about I make coffee, and you can get dressed?' he said.

'Fine,' she replied. She was still half asleep and followed him up the stairs. Adam went straight for the kitchen, and she stood in the middle of the lounge, feeling like a zombie.

'If you need a quick shower to help you wake up, go for it,' he said over his shoulder.

'Thanks,' she said and went to the bathroom. She tied her hair up in a ponytail so it wouldn't get wet and got in. As the hot water ran over her body, she remembered. Adam had offered to take her paddle boarding and meet some of his friends and their wives and spend the morning on the beach. She hadn't thought it would be quite so early, and she'd tried to push it out of her mind as she didn't really want to go in the sea and the idea of trying to balance on a paddleboard terrified her. It wasn't the thought of making a fool of herself, it was more than that, and she wasn't able to put it into words, not even to herself.

She pulled on some shorts and a t-shirt and went to join Adam in the kitchen.

'I have a confession,' she said hesitantly, closing her eyes as she spoke as she didn't want to see his reaction. 'I didn't bring any bathers, and the idea of paddleboarding terrifies me.'

'No worries,' he said. 'You don't have to go on the water, Richie's wife, Linda, hates the paddleboard, she usually hangs out on the beach.' Gemma opened her eyes and stared at him. There was no look of reproach or annoyance on his face. Until that moment, she hadn't realised how much she had been bracing for it. Harry had always pushed her to do things, to go out of her 'comfort zone', especially when it was something he wanted to do. It was never reciprocated, and he was likely to yell at her if she didn't want to participate. She had learned it was easier to go with his plans.

'Are you sure?'

'I'm sure,' he said handing her a reusable takeaway cup with coffee. 'The guys and I do this often and not everyone wants to go in the water. Scotty often sits and watches as he claims the water is too cold, unless we have a heat wave.' He laughed. Gemma felt better. She wasn't quite awake yet, but the coffee was helping and she marveled at this feeling of acceptance that she hadn't felt before.

'Let me get my hat and put on some shoes,' she said. She went to the bedroom, taking a deep breath before putting her sunhat, sunglasses, and sunscreen in her backpack and slipping some sandals on her feet. She had come to Sapphire Bay for an adventure, something different, and this ticked the boxes in a way she hadn't expected.

'Right, let's go,' she said. Adam smiled and they left her apartment to walk down and meet the others.

***

An hour and a half later, Adam, Richie, Benji and Benji's wife, Ireland, were walking up the beach after being out on their paddle boards. Gemma was sitting with Linda, Scotty, and Amanda, Scotty's partner, on the beach. As he paused to shake the water out of his hair, he looked at the scene in front of him. Gemma was sitting on a towel, a paper bag with, what he assumed, a hot egg and bacon roll in it. She was laughing with Linda about something, looking completely relaxed. He smiled before feeling an elbow in his ribs.

'What are you grinning about, Cooper?' Richie asked him.

'I wasn't grinning,' Adam tried to protest. Richie stared at him. 'Fine, I was thinking that Gemma looks like she fits in, it's nice.'

'Sure,' Richie raised an eyebrow. 'She looks like she fits in, is that all you were thinking?'

Adam knew exactly what Richie was implying and he wasn't going to go there.

'Leave it off, Richie,' Ireland said. 'They're friends.'

'Adam could do with a girlfriend, it's been too long,' Richie insisted.

Adam sped up, wanting to put some distance between himself and his friend. He didn't need this sort of teasing, especially as she was leaving Sapphire Bay in two weeks. He could hear Richie and Ireland bickering in a way that only old friends can. As he walked, he watched Gemma with the others. As far as he could see, there was no awkwardness in their interactions, and he wished that she was staying. He watched her laugh at something Scotty was saying and it hit him. He stopped suddenly with the realisation. He cared about Gemma and really hoped she'd stay. Even if they were destined to be friends only, he liked her. A lot.

'Oy, keep moving,' Benji said, bumping into him.

'Sorry,' Adam mumbled and kept moving. They joined the others and Gemma held out a paper bag to him.

'I think it's still hot,' she said. He took it and mumbled thanks, sitting next to her on a towel that was already spread out. He ate quietly, listening to the easy banter of the others.

'Oh, yes, you have to come to trivia on Tuesday night,' Linda was saying. 'These guys are rubbish.' Everyone laughed. 'Ireland, Amanda, and I don't always go, but we can make an exception next week.'

'Not that you girls being there helps,' said Scotty. 'We're still rubbish.'

'But it's fun,' said Ireland.

'Why would I make a difference?' Gemma asked.

'You're a history teacher, aren't you?' Scotty said. Gemma nodded. 'History is one of our worst areas, and Margaret, from the library, hosts the night, and I swear she chooses questions just so we'll lose!'

'You and your conspiracy theories,' Benji teased him. 'I'm sure it's not that.'

'Prove it,' Scotty said.

'Adam, don't you think Gemma should join us for trivia on Tuesday?' Linda asked him. He swallowed the last mouthful of his roll.

'That'd be good,' he said, trying to sound casual, but inside he had butterflies in his stomach at the thought of spending more time with Gemma, even though they were going to be spending time working on the carols presentation that weekend too.

'It's settled,' Linda said. 'You can join the Pack of Spuds on Tuesday night.' Adam liked how Gemma laughed at the name of their trivia group. Linda gave her all the details.

'Right,' Scotty said. 'We need to get a move on; we promised to head off to Mum and Dad's for lunch and could do with a shower to get all this sand off before we go.'

At that, the group started to pack up and say their goodbyes. Adam offered to walk Gemma back to her apartment.

'Your friends are really nice,' Gemma commented as they walked.

'Thanks,' Adam said. 'It's great that you can join us for trivia on Tuesday night.'

'It sounds fun,' she said. They fell into an easy silence, both lost in their own thoughts. Adam wanted to reach out and hold her hand as they walked, but thought it would be overstepping, so he held himself back.

'So, we still on to go through stuff for the presentation later?' Gemma asked when they got to her apartment. 'I could do with a rest before we start working, it was an early start.' Adam smiled at the twinkle in her eye.

'Sounds good,' he said. 'Around 3? I'll bring something for afternoon tea.'

'See you then.' He waited until she was inside before turning around and walking back to where he'd parked his car near the beach. Meeting his friends like this was something they did regularly, but the addition of Gemma made it feel different, as if their group had been missing something or someone they hadn't realised they were missing.

He wanted to kick himself with these thoughts. She was going home in two weeks. Not to mention he was a 52-year-old man, not a 18-year-old schoolboy with a crush.

'Get a grip, Cooper,' he said to himself as he drove home. 'She's a friend and colleague, nothing more.' But the feeling that he wanted something more wouldn't leave him alone.

Chapter 11

On Monday morning, Gemma practically floated into the library. She had had the most amazing weekend, even though waking early on Saturday wasn't in her plans. She had enjoyed spending time with Adam's friends on the beach and was looking forward to the trivia night the following evening. She and Adam had made good progress on the presentation, and she had a list of things to keep her eyes out for as she continued to archive all the material.

Gemma knew she had only been in Sapphire Bay for two weeks, but it felt like she had been here much longer. It was starting to feel like home, and that thought worried her. In two weeks, she was heading back to the city, to her real life.

'Happy Monday, Gemma,' Margaret greeted her cheerily. Today she was wearing a t-shirt that said 'My Christmas List: Books, Books, and More Books', and embellished with Christmas decorations and flying books.

'Morning, Margaret,' she replied.

'Those new archive boxes and folders have arrived for you,' Margaret said. 'I've put them in the storeroom for you.'

'Thank you,' A bubble of excitement rose up in Gemma and she clapped her hands. Margaret laughed.

'I haven't seen anyone so excited about stationery in… well, I don't know how long,' Margaret said. Gemma looked down in embarrassment. 'Don't get embarrassed,' Margaret said. 'I think it's pretty cool. I love a good stationery delivery.' Gemma looked up and met Margaret's eyes; a look passed between them and Gemma knew she'd found a kindred spirit.

'There's a special joy in knowing that you can get things organised,' Gemma said. 'Those boxes in the storeroom are so old they're falling apart.'

'It will be good to see things in some sort of order,' Margaret said. 'Have you found much treasure back there?'

Gemma told Margaret some of the things she had found, some of the stories she'd discovered. When she told her about a funny story she had seen in the local paper from a few decades ago when a huge gust of wind came through and blew Santa's hat from his head and a child on her father's shoulders caught it.

'That was me!' Margaret exclaimed. 'I was that child.'

'Really?' Gemma said. 'How did you manage to catch the hat?'

'I honestly don't know,' Margaret said. 'It came flying and I held out my hand and caught it. One of those lucky moments. A staff photographer from the paper caught the moment, and that's why it ended up in the Sapphire Bay Express.'

'Brilliant,' Gemma said. 'That's one of the moments we want to include in the presentation, the photo was one that made us laugh, the look of shock on your face.' Both women started laughing. 'I'd better keep moving, those boxes aren't going to unpack themselves.'

Gemma headed to the storeroom and let herself in. The scene was pure chaos, but she knew it would be. There were all the papers she'd been sorting out, broken archive boxes were at the back of the room ready to be taken to the recycling bin, and, in the middle, were the boxes of new stationery that had just been delivered. She looked at them and saw possibility everywhere. The neat rows of files and boxes all sorted ready to be digitised at some point in the future. An image flashed into her mind of a book or some other sort of exhibit showcasing the history of the carols. She shook her head to dismiss it. She was going home in two weeks, but all this work she was doing could pave the way to someone else continuing the project.

The thought of someone else coming in made her feel disappointed and this surprised her, but she pushed it away and started opening the boxes of stationery so she could get them organised, ready to be filled with archive material.

***

'Coffee break?' Adam asked, coming through the door later that afternoon.

'Um, sure, what time is it?' Gemma asked.

'It's after 3,' he replied. Gemma was in a corner of the storeroom, one she hadn't been able to access earlier, sitting in the midst of decorations, tulle, Santa hats, and fabrics in a variety of colours. 'What are you doing?' He put down the coffee cups he was carrying and went over to help her up.

'I think I've hit gold,' Gemma said. 'This looks like costumes and decorations and set dressings from the carols from I have no idea how long.'

'Cool?' Adam said. Gemma could tell he wasn't sure about this.

'Some of these could have been worn by Alf and Joan Trevors, or anyone else of note, if nothing else, they are a great insight into the event,' Gemma said, excitement building in her voice. 'I had a fleeting thought that the committee could do an exhibition next year to celebrate 70 years, and these would be amazing to display.' She picked up a dress that clearly needed mending. 'Depending on what sort of condition they're in.'

'Now, that is cool,' Adam said. 'So, what's the plan?'

'First we need to see what we have here,' Gemma said. Adam smiled.

'No, first, you need coffee. Have you had lunch?' Gemma looked down at her feet. 'I think I forgot to eat...'

'Then let's go to the bakery, if you're going to get through this, you need to eat,' Adam said. He led her out of the storeroom, the mugs of coffee abandoned on the table. As they walked to the bakery, Gemma told him about what she had found, pleased that he was getting as excited as she was. She had found some treasure, it wasn't quite what they had expected, but all of this would help when they did their presentation the following week.

Chapter 12

On Tuesday evening, Gemma reluctantly pulled herself away from work so she could shower and change before heading to the pub to meet Adam and his friends for the trivia night. She had been so immersed in the costumes and decorations as well as sorting out her files, she didn't want to leave. It didn't help that she was covered in dust from the boxes she was only just starting to sort.

When she was clean, she got dressed in a long flowing skirt and simple t-shirt and added the sunflower necklace she had bought from Ireland. The yellow of the sunflower perfectly complemented her navy t-shirt.

'Well, Gemma,' she addressed her reflection in the mirror. 'Let's do this.' It had been a long time since she'd made some new friends. Most of the ones she had were parents from when Joe and Sammy were at school, or she had met through work. This was the first time in, she couldn't remember how long she had spent time with people who liked her for who she was, not because of her children, or her role as history teacher. Here, she was simply Gemma. It was a new feeling for her, and she quite liked it.

***

'Gemma, over here!' She spotted Linda waving to her from a table near the edge of the room as she entered the pub. She waved back and weaved through the other tables. Linda was there with the others. 'Adam is at the bar,' Linda said when Gemma sat down. She hadn't realised she was looking for him.

'I like your necklace,' Ireland said. Gemma grinned.

'What can I say, I have great taste.' They laughed. 'I'm wishing I'd bought the fairy bread one too.'

'I'm sure I can arrange to get one you to,' Ireland replied.

'Here we go,' Benji appeared with Adam and Ritchie at his side. They put drinks on the table. 'We've ordered some chips and other nibbles too.'

'Thanks, love,' Ireland took a glass of wine as Benji kissed her.

'Sauvignon blanc?' Gemma looked up to see Adam had sat down in the chair beside her and was offering her a glass. She smiled.

'Thank you, you remembered.' Adam smiled.

Before they could say anything more, a horn sounded and the MC for the night stood up with a microphone at the front of the room. Gemma could see Margaret sitting behind her with pages of what she assumed were the trivia questions on them. Then it all started.

The night was full of joking, laughter, camaraderie, and occasionally getting questions right. By the end of the night, the Pack of Spuds came 9th and everyone celebrated because they had made the top 10. There were only 12 teams that night, but they all took it as a win.

'Did Margaret know Gemma was coming?' Scotty asked. 'There weren't many history questions tonight.'

'And not many to do with Christmas songs either,' Amanda said. 'What's going on there? I've been studying them.'

'I know!' Scotty groaned. 'If I ever have to hear *Good King Wenceslas* or *All I want for Christmas is You* again it will be too soon.' Amanda swatted his shoulder affectionately.

'So, did Margaret know?' Scotty asked again, looking pointedly at Adam.

'I didn't say anything,' said Adam.

'I may have,' Gemma said. 'I told her yesterday as I was leaving for the day, sorry guys.'

'Don't worry about it,' Adam put his arm around her shoulder. 'We couldn't have broken our tradition of trivia nights by winning something.'

The group was heading out to the carpark and Adam wasn't moving his arm from her shoulder. Gemma leaned in, enjoying the friendly moment. She had had a wonderful night with these new friends, and she didn't want the evening to end. Adam kept his arm around her shoulders until it came time to say farewell to his friends at their cars.

'Can I walk you home?' Adam asked. She knew his place wasn't close to hers but wasn't ready to part ways yet.

'That would be lovely,' she said. They started walking in silence, the space between them comfortable and neither felt like that had to say anything to fill the gap.

'Did you have a good night?' Adam asked when they were about halfway to her apartment.

'It was wonderful,' Gemma replied. 'Your friends are great.'

'They are,' Adam replied. 'Ireland was over the moon you wore her necklace.'

'She's really talented. Linda has invited me for coffee later in the week.'

'That's great,' Adam said. 'I think they think you're great too.' Gemma smiled in the darkness.

'It's a pity I'm leaving in just over a week and a half,' she said quietly, hoping he didn't hear it. She changed the topic to fill him in on some of the things she'd been doing that day, including finding a Christmas star with 1999 printed on it and a decoration of a toilet roll from 2020. This discussion filled in time until they got back to her apartment.

'Thanks for inviting me to trivia,' she said.

'I'm glad you came,' he said. 'That was the last one until January, between the carols next week, then Christmas and New Year, we take a break. The January ones are a bit different as many tourists join in, but they're still a lot of fun. Maybe you can come back for a few days without Margaret knowing and help us get even higher on the ladder.' She looked at his face. There was a mix of joking and hope.

'We'll see,' she said. 'See you tomorrow.'

'Night.'

She went inside her apartment and ran up to the balcony so she could watch him walk away. As he got to the end of the driveway, he turned and waved before heading the street.

Chapter 13

The rest of the week seemed to pass by in a blur of archive boxes, notes, watching videos and discovering interesting props. The storeroom was beginning to look more organised than organised chaos and Gemma was proud of what she had achieved in three weeks. She hadn't seen much of Adam after work as he had been busy with preparations for the Carols by Candlelight event, but she had gone out for dinner with Ireland, Linda, and Amanda on Thursday night.

It was now late on Saturday afternoon and Gemma and Adam had spent most of the day working on their presentation. She heard her phone ringing and scrambled to find it under the papers that were spread out on the dining table.

'Hello?' she said when she found it. She had been so frazzled she hadn't looked to see who it was.

'Mum?' the voice of Sammy came down the line.

'Sammy, sweetheart,' she said. She wasn't sure if she welcomed this interruption, especially as she hadn't heard much from her daughter since she'd been in Sapphire Bay. She started to wonder if there was some sort of emergency. 'Just hang on a minute,' she held the phone to her shoulder to muffle the sound. 'It's my daughter,' she said to Adam, almost apologetically.

'How about I go and get that pizza we were talking about while you're on the call,' Adam suggested. 'Give you some privacy.'

'Thanks, that sounds great,' she said and waited until he was heading down the stairs. 'Sorry about that sweetheart, how are you?'

'Was that a man's voice I heard?' Sammy said in a tone that transported Gemma back to the days when she was in high school. 'You're not that good at muffling the phone, you do know there is a mute option.'

'That was Adam, my coworker,' Gemma said. 'We're working on a presentation for the council on Monday.'

'Sure you are,' Sammy teased. Gemma rolled her eyes. She hadn't really dated anyone since her marriage ended and Sammy would occasionally put two and two together and somehow make seventeen when it came to interactions with men, assuming relationships that didn't exist and, on occasion, getting quite nasty about them.

'I'm sure that's not why you're calling,' Gemma wasn't in the mood for Sammy's teasing. She had to admit that it was a little too close to how she was starting to feel about Adam but wasn't ready to share that with anyone just yet.

'Fine,' Gemma could hear the tone in her daughter's voice that showed she wasn't impressed with the change in subject. 'I can't get the air conditioner working.' Gemma found herself relieved that the issue wasn't something more serious.

'Did you press the right buttons on the remote?'

'Yes,' there was a sigh of exasperation. 'It was working a couple of days ago.'

'Did you change the batteries?'

'What batteries?'

'In the remote,' Gemma said in her best patient mum voice.

'Right,' said Sammy. 'Um, where would I find new batteries?'

'In the box of batteries in the laundry cupboard.'

'Cool, I'll try that. If I don't call back, it's all sorted.' The call ended without Sammy saying goodbye. Gemma tossed her phone on the table and went out onto the balcony to look over the bay. It was so peaceful here and Gemma had been feeling more herself than she had in years. Her focus was on her work, she was making some new friends, she would spend evenings on the balcony with a glass of wine, some chocolate, and reading a book, when she wasn't out for dinner or working on the presentation.

Sammy's phone call had all but pulled her back into 'Mum Mode' and thoughts of her daughter trying to get the batteries into the remote control filled her mind. Going there made her feel different in a way she couldn't quite put her finger on. She knew that she would always be mum to Joe and Sammy, and always be there for them, but could she step away from that now and be simply Gemma? Before she could think about this more, a voice interrupted her musings.

'Rapunzel, Rapunzel, let down your hair,' Adam's voice floated up to her. She looked down and saw him standing there with two pizza boxes in one hand and a bag with garlic bread and drinks in the other. He had a cheeky look on his face. Gemma laughed.

'Sorry, my hair's a bit short, but I can open the door for you,' she called out before turning to go inside to let him in. She was still giggling as she opened the door. 'That smells great.'

'Then let's eat it before it gets cold,' he smiled at her. 'I also picked up some wine.'

'Great,' she led the way upstairs. 'Let's eat on the balcony.' She got some plates and glasses on her way through the living area, and they settled down to enjoy the sea breeze.

'Was everything okay at home?' Adam asked, then added when she looked confused. 'Your daughter on the phone.'

'Oh yes,' Gemma said. 'She couldn't get the air conditioner working.'

'That's important,' Adam said.

'I'm sure she would have worked it out eventually,' Gemma said. 'The remote just needed new batteries, I guess.' She paused and took a mouthful of pizza. 'This is really good.'

They fell into an easy silence for a while as they both enjoyed their meal.

'You know,' Gemma said, reaching for another slice. 'It's funny that not long ago, everything was about the kids. Now they're adults, it's not so much. Don't get me wrong, I love my children, but I'm not part of their lives any more.'

'You have two kids, right?' Adam said. They had spoken about their families and backgrounds, but not in any great detail.

'Yes, Joe is on the world's longest gap year, and Sammy is still at home, about to do her last year of university. Neither of them need me anymore, at least, not like they used to.'

'That makes sense, kids grow up and leave the nest,' Adam said.

'True, but Sammy seems in no hurry to leave,' Gemma laughed at the thought. 'It's convenient that we live so close to the university, what with the cost of living at the moment it's, well, convenient.' She shrugged as she repeated the word. 'Honestly, I feel a bit all at sea at the moment, one of the reasons I took the job here.'

'Is that a deliberate pun?' Adam asked with a wink.

'Not quite deliberate, but fitting,' Gemma said. 'I'm on long service leave from my teaching job. I love being a teacher, but feel like I need something different, and I don't want to climb the ladder, I love being with the students and I don't want that stress.' She hadn't admitted this to anyone, and she couldn't believe she was saying it to Adam.

'You could always move out of home,' he said with a teasing tone in his voice. Gemma stared at him.

'I couldn't do that,' she said. While she had entertained the thought of moving to Sapphire Bay, she had always dismissed it. She had responsibilities, to Sammy, to her students, didn't she?

'Why not?' Adam asked. 'One of the reasons I came back here was the city didn't have the right feel to it, especially after my marriage broke down. I tried to force it, but it didn't work. I used my dad's death as the catalyst to move, and this fits me better. Maybe where you are now doesn't feel like home anymore because you are a different person than you were. You're starting a new stage of life, a new you.'

'Maybe,' she said. She reached over to the table for a slice of pizza, only to find a seagull was beating her to it. She laughed and Adam joined in, once she pointed out the seagull flying away with the pizza.

'We'd better get back to the presentation,' Adam said when they'd stopped laughing. 'We have a pretty solid plan for a book too, but that would be a project for after Christmas.' He gathered the empty pizza boxes and plates and headed inside.

'But I won't be here after Christmas,' she said quietly, picking up the wine bottle and glasses. 'Or...' she stopped her mind at the thought. She was only here for another week, then she was back to her real life. After Christmas she would start preparing for the new school year and supporting Sammy through the final year of her degree. As she walked inside, she felt heavy with that thought, but that feeling lifted when she and Adam settled into their presentation planning again.

That night as she lay in bed, she thought about what Adam had said. Could she be the one to move out of home? What would that look like? The thoughts swirled in her mind as she drifted off to sleep.

Chapter 14

Monday was a day that showed how fickle the weather can be. Instead of calm, warm weather that Sapphire Bay had served up the last three weeks, it was cold and wet. Gemma hoped this wasn't a sign of things to come in the council meeting. Due to the rain, she drove to the library for the first time. As she drove, she thought about how much she had enjoyed spending time with Adam on Saturday and how she had missed him on Sunday as he was busy with preparations for the Carols by Candlelight this coming Thursday. She parked her car and ran inside before she got too wet.

'Good morning, Margaret,' she tried to sound upbeat and chirpy when she greeted the library assistant. She was full of nerves that she knew wouldn't die down until it was time for the council meeting.

'Good morning, Gemma,' Margaret said. Today, she was wearing what could only be described as an ugly Christmas sweater. It was cream with red and green snowflakes and Christmas trees, and on the front was a pile of books with a hand sticking up and the words *I'm Okay*.

'Nice jumper,' Gemma said.

'Thanks, my niece sent it to me from the US last year,' Margaret said. Gemma smiled and moved on to the storeroom, hoping that some time spent sorting and organising would help her feel less nervous.

As she entered the room, she paused and looked around, hardly able to believe it had been three weeks since she'd walked into this room for the first time. Where they had been a dusty mess, all the shelves were now clean. The broken archive boxes had been replaced with fresh, new ones, all clearly labelled. The boxes of costumes had been transformed and were now hanging on temporary racks with bedsheets draped over them to protect them from dust or in clear plastic tubs, all labelled so she knew was in them. There was still work to be done, and only five days to finish the job, but she had made a lot of progress. As she surveyed the room, Gemma felt proud of herself.

'Howdy partner,' Adam seemed to appear from nowhere.

'I'm seriously getting you a bell to wear around your neck as a Christmas present,' she joked. 'Or one of Margaret's Christmas t-shirts that has jingle bells on them.' He laughed.

'Are you ready for the presentation this afternoon?' he asked.

'I hope so,' she said.

'One more run through over lunch?'

'Yes, please,' she replied.

'Right, I'll pick up some burgers and see you back here around 1 so we can go through it all,' he said. 'Then we have time to go to the council chambers for the meeting at 3.'

'That sounds great,' she said. They said their goodbyes, and Gemma moved her focus to the latest folder of information she was sorting ready for archive. This one was from 1985 and the photographs were starting to fade, but they caught the joy of everyone involved and made Gemma smile.

***

Gemma shifted nervously in her seat. The council meeting was in progress and was moving slowly. The longer it went on, the more her nerves rose. Adam reached over and squeezed her hand gently and mouthed 'Soon'. She smiled a wonky smile at him, grateful that he seemed to understand how she was feeling. She had a hunch that he shared those feelings.

From the moment she had walked into the meeting room, she had felt out of place. She hadn't brought any business wear with her, so had chosen to wear a simple maxi skirt in swirling blues and a navy t-shirt as it was the closest thing she had to a professional outfit. She had been tempted to add the sunflower necklace, but thought it may be even more out of place, so she was wearing a simple chain with a silver heart pendant that Sammy had given her one Mother's Day. Adam was wearing a navy suit without a tie, and she couldn't help thinking how smart he looked. She hadn't seen him in a suit jacket before. He usually dressed in slacks and a shirt for work.

Then it was their turn. The mayor called out their names. Adam squeezed her hand again as they stood up.

'We've got this,' he said quietly as they made their way to the front of the room.

'We do,' she smiled, more confidently this time. She plugged the USB into the laptop and the first slide appeared on the big screen on the wall behind them.

'Good evening, everyone,' Adam began. 'Most of you know me, I'm Adam Cooper, and this is Gemma Duncan. We are here to tell you about the annual Sapphire Bay Carols by Candlelight event.'

'I was invited to archive all the documents from nearly 70 years of this event. In the process of sorting the archives, I could see how important this event is to the Sapphire Bay community through all that time. We want to share with you some of the things I have discovered and request the council review its plans for the redevelopment of the foreshore to ensure there is an event space, not only for the Carols by Candlelight, but also other fantastic events for the community.' Gemma found that her nerves went away as she warmed to her topic.

The slide changed to show copies of the earliest photographs she had found.

'Did you know that Carols by Candlelight in Sapphire Bay began in 1956, at that time, Sapphire Bay was a small community of around 500 residents. It was significant in that all the local churches joined together, something that didn't happen very often in those days. The local Anglican church wheeled their piano to the foreshore so residents could enjoy some carols together. The decision was made to have it on the foreshore as it was considered neutral territory,' Gemma told the crowd.

Adam and Gemma took turns telling stories throughout the years, high-lighting the importance of community, the economic impact of the event, and the cultural benefits. They shared one of the videos from the lockdown event in 2020 as well as many photos and scans of newspaper clippings.

'You see that the carols are much more than a fun event at Christmas, and how much the backdrop of the foreshore plays a part every year,' Gemma said.

'We would like the council to reconsider their plans for the foreshore to include space for events such as Carols by Candlelight,' Adam said.

'Along with the carols,' Gemma added. 'There have been other events held on the foreshore, such as community markets and music festivals. These have great economic impact as well as help to build community.'

'Are there any questions?' Adam asked, bringing their presentation to a close.

'I think we have everything we need,' the mayor said. 'You have certainly given us a lot to consider.' He flipped through the printed information

Gemma and Adam had prepared and handed out during their presentation. 'Now, on to other business.'

Gemma and Adam sat down, and Adam reached for her hand and squeezed it again.

'Well done,' he whispered.

'You too,' she said. She left her hand where it was in his. It felt good there.

Chapter 15

T he next morning, Gemma was still on a high from the council meeting. She knew there hadn't been any resolution, but she felt the mayor and the other counsellors had listened to their presentation. After the meeting, she and Adam had gone to the local Italian restaurant for a celebratory dinner.

She almost skipped into the library, glad that the weather had cleared up. It wasn't hot, but at least it wasn't raining. As she went past the beach, she looked over and was disappointed the paddle boarders weren't out, but figured it was probably a bit rough for them.

'Morning, Margaret,' she called out cheerily. Today, Margaret was wearing a t-shirt with the slogan 'All I want is books', which seemed plain compared to some of her other t-shirts, however the light up antlers on her head added a sparkle.

'Morning, Gemma,' Margaret replied. 'So, how did it go?'

'I think it went well,' Gemma said. 'There were no tech issues, so that's a plus.'

'I know you were worried about that,' said Margaret. 'What's next?'

'Well, wait for a response, I guess,' said Gemma. 'Though my task for the next few days is to get the storeroom completely sorted, or at least as much as possible. My contract ends on Friday.'

'Already?' said Margaret. 'I'll miss having you around, and I know Adam will too.' Gemma admitted that she would miss both Margaret and Adam too, but it was a four-week contract. She said goodbye and moved to the storeroom. Once inside, she put herself to work to distract herself from the fact she had only four days left in this job. She was due to go home on Saturday. At least she would be here for the Carols by Candlelight on Thursday night.

She heard the door to the storeroom open, and she turned to see Adam coming in.

'Morning,' she said with a sly smile on her face. 'You weren't able to creep up on me this time.'

'Who's creeping?' Adam said with a tone that was a cross between disappointment and amusement. 'Last night went well.'

'It did. We spoke about it last night over dinner, remember,' Gemma gently teased. Adam grinned back at her. 'I can't believe this is coming to an end,' Gemma said quietly, thinking about all the times Adam had surprised her by coming in to the room without her noticing. She was going to miss that.

'We still have a book to produce,' Adam said. Gemma looked at him, surprised, she hadn't realised he had heard her.

'I don't think we can do that in three and a half days,' Gemma replied. 'I'm going home on Saturday.'

'Hmmm,' Adam said noncommittally. They hadn't spoken about her going home, instead, preferring to be in the moment. Gemma had enjoyed their easy friendship and spending time with his friends. She felt like he saw her for who she was, not her being a mother or any of the other myriad roles she had in her life. She could be herself around him. His quiet teasing was something she enjoyed and was able to give back without worrying that he would get angry with her.

'What are your plans for the day?' Adam asked.

'Continuing to sort all this out,' Gemma said. 'Not sure I'll get it all done before Friday, but I'll do my best.'

'Sounds like a plan, I'll leave you to it,' Adam said. 'I'd better get back to my real job,' he had a joking tone in his voice that didn't quite hit the mark. 'Dinner after work?'

'Two nights in a row, I am a lucky girl,' Gemma tried to joke back. 'Fish and chips on the foreshore, if the weather holds?'

'It's a date,' he said and left the room before the impact of those words set in.

Did he mean it's a date as in an appointment on the calendar, or a date as in something more? She mused. She shook her head. Surely he was using it as just a saying, nothing more. She turned to the boxes she was sorting and tried to forget about it.

***

Adam left the storeroom and headed back upstairs to his desk, the glow from the council meeting slowly giving way to a more complicated feelin g.Gemma would be leaving Sapphire Bay on the weekend.

The thought followed him up the stairs.

Over the past few weeks, she had slipped into his days more easily than he would have expected. He thought about the way they'd fallen into conversation so naturally, the laughter at trivia night, the way she fitted in with his friends as if she'd always been part of the group. He thought about her standing beside him at the council meeting, calm and capable, speaking with such quiet confidence.

And the way she laughed at his jokes, properly laughed, as if they actually mattered.

He sat at his desk and let out a slow breath. He was going to miss her.

That realisation landed harder than he expected. He hadn't gone into any of this thinking it would mean anything more than a temporary project, a few shared coffees, some good company. Somewhere along the way, though, it had started to feel... different. Easier. Warmer. Something he hadn't realised he'd been missing.

He turned on his computer, trying to focus on his work, but the thought stayed with him. By the end of the day, he decided, he would say something, nothing dramatic, just that he'd like to stay in touch. He didn't want to put pressure on her or change what they had, but he also didn't want to pretend that the last few weeks hadn't mattered.

Because they had.

***

That evening as she walked to the foreshore with Adam, she reflected on the last few weeks. She felt at peace in Sapphire Bay. The friends she'd made, especially Adam and Margaret, were the sorts of friends she'd been missing. Until that moment, she hadn't realised how isolated she'd become.

Would moving here be something she could do? Amanda had commented that the local high school was looking for a history teacher, she worked there teaching Maths and Science. Was it too close to the start of the year to apply for something? And what about Sammy? Gemma knew her daughter was technically an adult, but she still lived at home. And if she quit her job, would they be able to find a new teacher to fill her place?

'You seem a million miles away,' Adam's voice broke through her thoughts.

'I'm just thinking,' she said.

'Careful, it might become a habit,' he joked and she knocked his shoulder with hers. 'Anything you want to share?' he asked more seriously.

'I was just thinking this is such a beautiful place,' Gemma said. 'And what a wonderful time I've had in Sapphire Bay.'

'It certainly is a wonderful place,' said Adam. 'And we've enjoyed having you here.'

'I'll miss it when I'm back in the city,' she said quietly.

'Just the town?' he asked. Gemma wasn't sure if he was teasing or if this was a serious question. She decided to reply with a lighthearted answer.

'Well, there are pretty good fish and chips here,' she quipped as they went into the fish and chip shop.

As they sat on the foreshore eating their dinner, they moved on to other topics, especially the Carols by Candlelight event on Thursday night. Gemma was really looking forward to attending. Gemma couldn't get thoughts of moving to Sapphire Bay out of her mind, no matter how she tried.

When she got back to her apartment, she started doing some research to see if there were any teaching jobs available, even a temporary contract could be one way to see if this would work. An added bonus would be that she would return to Sapphire Bay and start working on the book to celebrate the 70th anniversary of the carols with Adam... and, of course, getting to know Adam more.

Chapter 16

·▾·♥·♥·♥·♥·

Thursday night was warm and clear. There was a soft wind blowing from the sea and a buzz of excitement in the air. Adam was going to be busy backstage and had arranged to meet up with Ireland, Amanda, and Scotty, and some of their teenage children, to watch the performance. Ritchie was at the gate handing out programs and would join them when the show began, and Benji was part of the band. Linda was helping the students from Sapphire Bay Secondary College get ready for their performance. Gemma spotted Ireland madly waving when she caught her eye.

Gemma made her way through the crowd and nearly bumped into Margaret. She was wearing a reindeer onesie, complete with face painted whiskers and a red nose. Gemma tried not to laugh.

'Hey there, watch where you're going,' Margaret laughed. 'Can't have Rudolph getting injured before the big day.' Gemma joined in the laughter.

'Certainly not,' she said. 'You on your own?'

'Nah,' Margaret said. 'I'm over there with my daughter, son-in-law, and the grandbaby, it's her first Christmas. My husband, Derek, is backstage somewhere.'

'It's wonderful that they can bring the baby,' Gemma said. Part of her wished she'd invited Sammy or Sarah and her family down to enjoy the event. She thought they'd enjoy it, but another part was glad to be there on her own with her new friends. *Maybe next year*, the thought popped into her head, taking her by surprise.

'I'm over there with some friends, so I'll see you later, enjoy the evening.' Gemma continued through the crowd to sit on a picnic rug with her friends. She felt a glow of warmth as they welcomed her as if she had been in Sapphire Bay longer than four weeks.

The lights went up on the temporary stage that had been placed on the foreshore and the noise of the crowd hushed as the MC walked on stage to begin proceedings.

As the night went on, Gemma marveled at the talent from the area. From the primary school choir who sang *Away in the Manger* and *Jingle Bells*, to the high school band performing *Santa Claus is Coming to Town* and *The Twelve Days of Christmas* with some talented students on vocals, and a myriad of puppets that the students had made to represent the various gifts. To the local bands coming on to perform some carols and a local author recited a Christmas poem he had written especially for the occasion. There were jokes and banter from various presenters, and when a seagull landed on the stage, no one bat an eyelid.

The sun went down during the performance and hundreds of battery-operated candles, that had been handed out as people arrived, lit up, adding to the magic of the scene.

Gemma was glad she was sitting with her friends. Every now and again, Ireland would nudge her to share a laugh at a funny comment from the MC. Amanda would regularly pass around platters of snacks or drinks she had in an esky. Ritchie would try to join in all the carols, singing off-key at the top of his voice and the others trying to get him to be quiet. Gemma felt a glow of belonging she hadn't realised she'd missed.

Gemma was almost sad when the audience was invited to join in singing *We Wish You A Merry Christmas* at the end of the night. She stood up with everyone else, waving her candle around and sang as loudly as she dared. It had been a wonderful evening.

As the crowds started leaving, Gemma sat back and watched her friends head to the stage to find their partners and help with the pack up. Gemma wasn't quite sure what to do, but she had promised Adam she would hang around to touch base with him before she went home. She moved to sit on a park bench on the foreshore to be out of the way of the people heading home and to wait for him.

'What did you think?' Gemma jumped at the sound of Adam's voice. She had been watching the stage and had no idea how he had come over without her noticing.

'Seriously, bells!' Gemma joked. 'It was fantastic, I loved every minute of it.' Adam sat down beside her.

'I only have a few minutes before going to help with the bump out, but I wanted to see you... um, see what you thought.' He repeated.

'I can see why you're so passionate about keeping this in the community,' Gemma said. 'This setting, it couldn't possibly be better, it's positively magical.'

She watched the people who were milling around, some were near the stage already starting to pack things up. There were parents trying to drag their children home, there were couples walking hand in hand. There were volunteers already starting to clean up the rubbish. She noticed Linda with some of her students who were obviously on rubbish duty and waved, her mind briefly taking her back to her school days.

'I'm glad you see it,' Adam said, bringing her back to the present.

'I hope we did enough to convince the council to include it in their plans,' Gemma replied. 'I'm surprised they didn't, especially given the mayor gave a speech during the event.'

'Me too,' Adam said. 'We can only cross our fingers and hope.'

They sat silently for a moment, Gemma felt at peace and she wanted to move her hand closer to his, and for a heartbeat, she thought she saw him glance her way as if he'd felt it too, but something stopped her. She had a flash of feeling. This is where she wanted to be. She had no idea if Adam felt the same, but she wanted to get to know him more.

'I'm really happy you came to Sapphire Bay,' Adam said quietly. Gemma wasn't quite sure she heard, but replied, 'Me too.'

'Hey, Adam, come and help, you slacker!' a joking voice cut through the moment. Gemma looked over and saw Adam looking at her with an expression she couldn't quite make out.

'Coming,' he turned to where the voice came from. 'I'd better go and help, will I see you tomorrow?'

'Should do,' said Gemma. 'Last day at the library, I head home on Saturday.'

'Then I'll be sure to look you up tomorrow,' he said. He hesitated and Gemma wondered if he was going to kiss her, but then he turned and was soon lost in the crowd packing up the stage.

As she watched him disappear into the crowd, she wondered if she should invite Adam and the others to her apartment for farewell drinks the next night. Something casual to mark the weeks she'd spent in Sapphire Bay and the friends she'd made. When he was out of sight, Gemma got up and walked back to her apartment.

Chapter 17

On Saturday morning, Gemma woke up earlier than she'd hoped. It was going to be her last day in Sapphire Bay and, while she wanted to enjoy it, she also didn't want to be awake early.

With the early start, she made herself a coffee and started packing up her belongings. Each item she folded felt heavier. She really didn't want to be going home, but she knew she couldn't stay here, even though she'd been having nagging thoughts about moving.

The sound of the doorbell took her by surprise, and she went downstairs to open the door.

'Good morning,' Adam's cheerful voice lifted her spirits.

'Good morning,' she replied. 'What are you doing here?'

'Have you had breakfast yet?' Gemma shook her head.

'Well, come on, I'm taking you out.'

'You're what?' she stumbled over her words. 'I have packing to do, and food in the pantry I need to eat so I don't have to take it home.' He laughed at her response.

'Please?' he said. 'Come to breakfast.' She just looked at him. 'I'll get you back in time to pack things up, I'll even help... do you trust me?'

His words transported her back to the time when Sammy had been obsessed with the *Aladdin* movie and had nearly worn out a DVD watching it over and over again. She closed her eyes and took a breath.

'Yes, just give me a minute to get my shoes and bag.' He followed her upstairs as she got her things ready. Together they walked out of the apartment and started heading down to the street.

'Where are we going?' she asked when he led her down a path towards the beach instead of towards the cafés in town.

'You'll see,' he said mysteriously. 'Now, close your eyes and hold onto my arm.' She eyed him cautiously before doing as she was told. He led her around a corner.

'Surprise!!!' Gemma opened her eyes. In front of her, in a rotunda with a barbecue and picnic tables, were her friends. Benji and Ireland, Ritchie and Linda, Scotty and Amanda, and even Margaret and Derek and a few other people she had met during her time in Sapphire Bay.

'Oh, wow,' Gemma exclaimed.

'We couldn't let you head back to the big smoke without a proper send off,' Ritchie said as Linda handed her a latte in a takeaway cup. Benji was at the barbecue cooking bacon and eggs, Amanda was arranging plates and sauces on a picnic table. Margaret was fussing over a gingerbread house. Adam stood there with a huge grin on his face.

***

The brunch was well underway. It had been late in the afternoon the day before when Adam realised he couldn't let Gemma just slip away without saying goodbye properly. He had sent a text to Linda who had helped rally the troops to put on this surprise brunch.

'Now for the presents,' Ritchie called over the chatter. That was something Adam hadn't expected. He watched his friends hand over parcels. A fairy bread necklace from Ireland and Benji. A book-themed Christmas t-shirt from Margaret's stash. A Sapphire Bay calendar for the following year from Ritchie and Linda. A bottle of wine from Scotty and Amanda. Gemma was gushing over all of them, and he saw some tears in her eyes.

'What about you?' Ritchie asked Adam.

'Hey, this whole thing was my idea, isn't that enough?' he did his best to sound light-hearted, at the same time kicking himself that he hadn't thought to give her a gift.

'Guess that'll do,' Ritchie said. 'We should start thinking about packing this all up…'

Adam watched Gemma joke and chat with his friends and felt the unmistakable hollow of a Gemma-shaped space forming in the group. He realised just how much her presence had changed the rhythm of their days; how easy and warm it had felt to have her around. They would all miss her.

He interrupted his thoughts to help pack things away and watched everyone hug Gemma and exchange promises to keep in touch. Linda mentioned that the secondary school was a wonderful place to work, and Adam felt a twinge of disappointment when Gemma dismissed the idea.

Once everything was put away, Adam and Gemma walked together to her apartment.

'It's going to be weird without you here,' Adam said as they walked up the road.

'What do you mean by that?' Gemma asked. Adam was startled; he thought he had said that in his mind, not out loud.

'Just…' he struggled to find the words. 'Just that I'll miss you.'

Gemma was quiet for a moment, and he feared he had overstepped.

'I'll miss you too,' she said. 'Especially your corny jokes.' Adam grinned at her effort to make the moment lighter.

'Is that all?' he asked as they got to her door.

'And maybe your help to get things in order here…'

'I haven't done that yet,' he said.

'Well then,' she said and Adam saw the twinkle in her eyes. He really did like the way she teased him and he would miss that.

A couple of hours later they had everything packed and the apartment was cleaned. He helped her pack the car and watched her put the key in the lockbox.

'I guess that's it,' Gemma said, leaning against her car.

'I guess so,' Adam said. 'I have really enjoyed getting to know you, please keep in touch, and come back to visit.' He hoped he wasn't sounding too desperate. As she opened the car door, he felt a flicker of longing, wishing there was more time.

'I will,' she said. She reached up to give him a hug. 'I've enjoyed getting to know you too.'

The hug ended and she got in her car to drive home. Adam watched her from the end of the driveway. He felt the emptiness settle around him as he took in the quiet street, and the space she had left behind. He hoped this wasn't the last he'd see of Gemma Duncan.

Chapter 18

· ♥ · ♥ · ♥ · ♥ ·

When Gemma got home that Saturday evening, she had been happily surprised to find that Sammy had decorated the Christmas tree and the house was looking tidy, if a little dusty, with a few dishes in the sink. For the first time in years, Gemma realised she didn't have a lot to do in the lead-up to Christmas. Most of her shopping had been completed in Sapphire Bay, and she and Sammy were going to Sarah's house for Christmas Day.

On Christmas Eve, Gemma stood back and looked around the lounge-room. The Christmas tree was the same one they had put up every year since Joe and Sammy were small, lights twinkling and reflecting off the tinsel. The decorations were a mix of childhood creations and ones collected over the years. It could never be called Insta-worthy, but it made her smile. Sammy had done a good job decorating it.

Underneath were presents wrapped for family members. A package had arrived from Joe, who was now in Switzerland for a white Christmas. She was looking forward to seeing what he had sent. A bigger surprise had been a gift from Adam that had arrived by mail earlier that day, now sitting under the tree.

Her gaze drifted around the room. The walls were covered with family photographs and a few prints. She tipped her head to one side, staring at a print of a beach, and memories of Sapphire Bay came flooding back. She allowed herself a few moments of thought before turning to take in the rest of the room. Near the Christmas tree as her old couch, one that had been purchased for convenience rather than comfort. The couch was fine, but not something she would have chosen if she'd had the time, money, or headspace when she'd bought it.

The air conditioner hummed softly, filling the warm, slightly stuffy room. Opening the windows didn't help to cool the room, and the faint noise from the main road, just a block away, reminded her how different home was from the quiet sea breeze in Sapphire Bay. She missed it already.

'Ready for Carols by Candlelight?' Sammy said brightly, entering the room with a tray of Christmas snacks, including some leftover gingerbread house pieces Margaret had insisted she take home.

'In a minute,' Gemma said. 'You set up the TV; I'll bring the wine.'

Gemma went to the kitchen. She and Sammy sat and watched the carols on television every Christmas Eve. As she got the bottle out of the fridge and two wine glasses, she noticed the Christmas bells that were hanging in a garland above the kitchen windows and had a sudden urge to text Adam. She hoped the gift she'd put in the mail on Monday had arrived, especially as it included an old cow bell she had spotted in a gift shop. They had been texting regularly and she missed him. Texting was fine, but it wasn't the same as enjoying a glass of wine together on the balcony or fish and chips on the foreshore. She sighed and went back to the loungeroom, pouring the wine before settling onto the couch.

Settling onto the couch with two glasses and the bottle in hand, Gemma smiled at her memories of Sapphire Bay and, especially, thoughts of Adam.

'Hey, what are you smiling about?' Sammy asked, settling beside her.

'Nothing,' Gemma said, turning her attention to the television.

The show started, and she found herself comparing the polished tele-vised performances with the magical experience in Sapphire Bay: the setting sun over the water, the hum of the crowd, the hundreds of little battery-operated candles. She could almost hear Ireland's laugh, Amanda handing out snacks, Ritchie singing off-key, and Adam moving behind the stage, helping make everything run smoothly. The memory made her smile again, bittersweet this time.

'Stop it,' she muttered to herself. 'You're home with your daughter. Enjoy the tradition, enjoy the moment.' But her thoughts kept drifting back, to Adam, Sapphire Bay, and the friends she'd made there.

Later that night, she couldn't sleep. Reaching for her laptop, still on the bedside table, she scrolled through job listings once more. A few positions seemed to match what she wanted, starting in term one. Could this really work? Did even thinking about it make her mad?

She fell asleep with her laptop beside her, still open on the page for vacancies at Sapphire Bay Secondary College, including a maternity leave replacement position for a history teacher, the small glow of possibility keeping her dreams warm.

Chapter 19

•·♥·♥·♥·♥·♥·

Boxing Day in Sapphire Bay was beautiful. It wasn't too hot and the bay was in perfect condition for paddleboarding. Adam joined Richie, Benji and Ireland on the water before joining the others at the rotunda for breakfast. These gatherings were something the group of friends did regularly, and Boxing Day brunch had become a tradition over the years. Adam couldn't help but think back to just over week ago when they had met here to farewell Gemma.

Adam found himself sitting a little way apart from the others, staring out over the water thinking about Gemma and wishing she was there with them.

'What's up, mate?' Scotty asked him.

'I'm fine,' Adam said. Scotty raised an eyebrow.

'Really, how are you?' Scotty repeated. 'Missing Gemma?' Adam stared at his friend.

'Is it that obvious?'

'Yep,' said Scotty.

'I just feel like something's missing today,' Adam began. 'I mean, we're all together as we are often, but Gemma isn't here. I can't put my finger on why, but....'

'You miss her,' Scotty said. 'I get it. You remember when Ireland went to that business conference in Melbourne last year.'

'Not quite the same,' Adam said. 'After all, you'd been married to her for over a decade, so I understand how much you'd miss her. I've only known Gemma for,' he paused to work it out. 'Only about a month, and we're just friends. It makes no sense to me.'

'It does to me,' said Scotty. 'It's okay to miss her. She might come back again.'

'Maybe,' said Adam.

'Or you could follow her to the city.'

'I don't think so, I don't think I could leave all of this.' Adam indicated the view as well as his friends.

'The city isn't that far away,' Scotty said. 'It's early days, I'm sure you'll meet up again. Now come and get yourself some food before Ritchie eats it all.'

Adam smiled and thanked his friend for understanding. They joined the rest of their friends. Adam still felt there was something missing but was able to relax enough to enjoy the company of his friends.

Later that afternoon, his heart soared as he received a text message from Gemma. It wasn't anything life changing, just a photo of her sister's pet cat playing with the wrapping paper after they had opened presents. He smiled and replied with a photo of a couple of magpies that had landed in his backyard. He liked that they were able to do this, send each other messages just because without having to say anything.

He stared at his phone wishing she was still in Sapphire Bay. The idea of a conversation about nothing much while sipping wine and watching the sunset filled him with longing. He promised himself to contact her after the New Year and invite her back for a visit. Maybe for the next foreshore market, if he couldn't think of any other occasion.

Chapter 21

⋅ ♥ ⋅ ♥ ⋅ ♥ ⋅ ♥ ⋅ ♥ ⋅

A few days later, Gemma was sitting with Sarah on Sarah's back porch with a glass of wine. Sammy had gone out somewhere with her friends and Sarah's kids had gone to the cricket with Kevin, Sarah's husband. They were all crazy about cricket.

'Enjoying being home?' Sarah asked. They had seen each other on Christmas day, but it wasn't time for any meaningful discussion.

'I'm not sure,' Gemma said. 'I'm missing Sapphire Bay.'

'Sapphire Bay… or Adam?' Sarah teased. Gemma bought some time to think by taking a sip of wine followed by a mouthful of Christmas cake.

'Maybe both?' Gemma said, not quite sure which she was missing more.

'Tell me,' Sarah said, inviting Gemma to explain. This was a change from a month ago when Sarah had all but accused Gemma of running away when she took the job at Sapphire Bay, she had definitely said that Gemma had lost her mind.

'Well…' Gemma began. 'I liked who I was when I was there.' These were thoughts Gemma hadn't put into words before, and she wasn't sure if they made sense. 'I was me; I wasn't Sammy and Joe's mum; I wasn't Harry's ex-wife. I wasn't the history teacher at the high school; I was just me.' She took a sip of wine. 'Almost everyone here knows me in relation to my children, or my work. I love my job, but I've been at the same school for so long. I know I don't want to be head of department or a principal, but

I feel like I'm ready for a new challenge. I also made new friends there, something I haven't done in years.'

'Sure you don't need a fancy sports car for your midlife crisis?' Sarah teased. Gemma shot her a look.

'I'm trying to be serious here.' Gemma said. Sarah had the good grace to look embarrassed. 'Somehow I found something in Sapphire Bay that I didn't even know I was looking for.'

'Sorry, sis,' Sarah said. 'Sounds like you are ready for a change. And maybe romance.' Gemma stuck her tongue out at her sister before replying.

'I think I am, at least for the change, and I think I've been feeling this way for longer than I realised,' Gemma said. 'Going to Sapphire Bay was the change I needed to help me see that.'

'And romance?' Sarah prompted.

'We'll see,' replied Gemma.

'What are you going to do now?'

'I have been looking at jobs,' Gemma said quietly. Saying it out loud made it seem real, that it was something she might be able to do.

'Have you applied for any?' Gemma stared at her sister.

'I don't know if I'm brave enough,' she began.

'If you need a change, then take it,' Sarah said. 'You are certainly brave enough, you did that when you applied for the job before Christmas, you are still brave now.'

'Since when have you been the impulsive one, and the one with good advice?' Gemma said.

'I'm not impulsive, but sometimes I do have good advice, though I don't know where it comes from.' The sisters laughed at that.

'I guess I could always apply,' Gemma said. 'What about Sammy? It's her final year of university.'

'As you said before you went away before, Sammy is a big girl, she can look after herself. It's not as if you're moving to Mars.' The sisters laughed again.

'But am I running away? Not facing things here?' Gemma was suddenly hit with feelings of guilt and uncertainty.

'Honestly, you don't sound like someone running away,' Sarah said. 'You sound like you're running towards something. Go for it, apply for the job and see what happens. Plus, you know what the best bit could be?'

'What?'

'Adam!' Sarah said with a twinkle in her eye.

Gemma poked her tongue out at her sister, like they had when they were kids and Sarah had said something to provoke her, then she quickly changed the subject. She missed Adam and was having fun sending him text messages. If she thought about it, being closer to him would be a definite benefit of moving to Sapphire Bay.

Chapter 22

· ♥ · ♥ · ♥ · ♥ · ♥ ·

New Years Eve was quiet at Gemma's house. Sammy was out at a party, Gemma hadn't been able to work out what her daughter's plans were, only to not wait up. Gemma settled down to watch the Christmas Eve concert from the Sydney Opera House, waiting for the midnight fireworks so she could go to bed. She hadn't felt like going out, at least not to anywhere local.

'Right, I'm going to do this,' she said to the sparkling Christmas tree in the corner of the room. 'I am going to apply for those jobs.'

She opened her laptop and brought up the job advertisements. There were two jobs that appealed to her, both were maternity leave positions. She figured that a short contract could be a way to test the waters and see if it was worth making a permanent move to Sapphire Bay. The first was a specialist history teacher and the second was under the broader humanities banner. It had been a long time since she'd taught anything other than history, but she figured she could always learn what she didn't know. When they had met for coffee in Sapphire Bay, Linda had talked about her work at the school and how the community was supportive, so she kept that in mind.

She looked over the requirements and dusted off her resume. She smiled as she added her job as archivist for the Sapphire Bay Carols by Candlelight.

When she was happy with her cover letter and resume, she took a deep breath, a sip of her wine, and pressed send.

'If I don't get either of them, it's a sign to change things up here,' she said to the Christmas tree. She tried convincing herself that it didn't really matter, but it did. It mattered more than she wanted to admit. The thoughts of moving and seeing that gorgeous view of the bay every day crowded her mind, along with thoughts of Adam mingled with thoughts of the friends she'd made.

She focused her thoughts on Adam. Had she imagined there may be something there, something more than friendship? It had been nearly 20 years since her marriage had ended and she had been on a few dates, but nothing that would even pretend to be a relationship in that time. She had been too busy with the kids and working to have the energy to pursue anything seriously.

She picked up her phone and sent a text message to Adam.

You won't believe what I've done... I've applied for a couple of jobs at Sapphire Bay Secondary.

She had barely pressed send when the phone rang. She smiled when she saw who was calling and answered.

'You've done what?' Adam's voice came down the phone, no greeting, just right to the point. Gemma laughed.

'I have applied for a couple of jobs at Sapphire Bay Secondary College,' she said. 'No idea if I'll get them, but I figured it wouldn't hurt to apply.'

'I'm crossing fingers and toes for you, it'd be great to have you here,' Adam said. Gemma got the feeling he was holding back some of his enthusiasm. 'I'll have to tell the others, and if you're in Sapphire Bay, we can work on the book and the exhibition for the anniversary.'

'Slow down,' Gemma laughed. 'Please don't tell the others, at least not yet. I haven't even told Sammy I was going to apply. I had almost forgotten about the book.'

'You hadn't,' Adam put on a mocked shocked tone making Gemma laugh again.

'You got me, I hadn't,' she said. 'I was teasing, and it will be great to keep working with you.'

'Hey, Adam, your turn for the next round,' she heard someone's voice in the background.

'Was that Benji?' Gemma asked.

'Yep, I'd better get back to them.'

'Wish everyone a happy New Year from me,' she said.

'Will do,' he said and they ended the call. Gemma put her laptop on the coffee table and her phone beside it. She curled up on the couch and tried to focus on the concert, but her mind kept pulling her back to Sapphire Bay and imagining what Adam, Benji, Ritchie, Ireland, Linda, Amanda, and Scotty were up to at the pub and wishing she was there with them.

***

'I'll be there in a minute,' Adam called to Benji as he hung up the phone to Gemma. Something bubbled inside him and all he wanted to do was jump up and down and dance like a mad thing and scream 'She's coming back!'. Instead, he fist pumped the air a few times saying 'YES!' quietly.

It took a few moments for him to calm himself before joining his friends, via the bar to order another round of drinks. He had no idea how he was going to keep this news to himself. He knew Gemma didn't have the job yet, after all it was nearly 11pm on New Years Eve, but there was hope.

He sat down beside Ritchie and tried to pretend the call from Gemma was simply to wish them all a happy new year.

Chapter 23

Gemma hadn't seen Sammy for a couple of days when she staggered into the kitchen for breakfast on January second.

'Good morning, sweetheart,' Gemma said, trying to contain her surprise. 'Happy New Year.' Sammy sat at the table opposite her and put her head in her hands. 'Coffee?'

'Most definitely,' Sammy mumbled, at least, that's what Gemma thought her daughter had said. It was hard to make out the words with her head buried in her arms. Gemma got up and went to the coffee machine. While it was doing its thing, she poured some water in a glass and got some paracetamol for her daughter. Sammy lifted her to take them and smiled gratefully. 'That was one big party,' she commented.

'Only one?' Gemma asked. Sammy started counting on her fingers.

'Okay, so three, maybe four? I can't quite remember.' Sammy put her head back down on her hands.

'Oh, to be young again,' Gemma said. The coffee was now ready, and she placed the mug in front of Sammy. She couldn't help thinking that, when she was Sammy's age, she was preparing for her wedding to Harry, and Joe wasn't that far away.

Gemma sat down again and ate her own breakfast.

'Sammy, there is something I need to talk to you about,' she began when she judged her daughter was a bit more awake and slightly less hungover.

'Hmm,' Sammy said, seeming to be more interested in what was on her phone than anything her mother was saying.

'I have applied for a couple of jobs in Sapphire Bay,' Gemma said. Sammy's head shot up from her phone, followed by a groan of pain and her holding her head.

'You've done what?'

'Applied for a couple of jobs, teaching at the secondary school down there,' Gemma started to feel less confident about the decision than she had on New Years Eve. Adam had been in regular touch with messages of support and encouragement, and she had been feeling this was the right move, until that moment when Sammy groaned.

'What about your current job?' Sammy asked. 'What about me?'

'The school will cope,' Gemma said. 'They have waiting lists of teachers who want to work there, I'm sure they have temporary teachers who can cover while they find someone to replace me. It has an excellent reputation. As for you, what about you?'

'Where will I live?' Sammy asked and Gemma was reminded, once again, that Sammy had her own life and her role was to provide her with a roof over her head. 'It's my last year of uni, I need...'

'Hang on a minute,' Gemma said, cutting her off. 'Firstly, I've only just applied, I haven't got a job yet. Secondly, they are short term positions, I won't be selling this house, at least not yet. I'm honestly not sure what the future will hold. And thirdly, you're an adult, I'm sure you'll find a place if you need to.'

'But...' Sammy started to protest, then stopped.

'But?'

'You'll move?'

'I expect so,' said Gemma. 'If I get the job. I figure a short-term contract would be best to start with. You see, I've never lived on my own before...'

'I'll say it again,' Sammy said. 'What about me?'

'What about you?' Gemma asked. 'As you pointed out, you're in the last year of university. The fact I haven't seen you since you went out on New Years Eve, nearly three days, and you were absolutely fine when I spent four weeks in Sapphire Bay tells me that you can live quite capably on your own. You are an amazing human being and things will work out. It's not as if Sapphire Bay is all that far away either. It's not the other side of the world.'

Sammy's phone beeped before they could say anything else. Sammy typed on her phone before getting up.

'Thanks for the coffee, I'm going to have a quick shower. Daniel is coming to pick me up in 20 minutes and we're meeting some friends for brunch.'

Gemma shot her a look to say she had just proven her point; she wasn't sure if Sammy understood.

Half an hour later, Gemma was sitting at the kitchen table, doing the crossword in the newspaper, Sammy paused and kissed her mother on the top of her head.

'All the best with the job, I hope you get it,' Sammy said, then rushed out the front door to meet her friend. Gemma stood up and put the kettle on for a fresh cup of tea. Part of her wished she was rushing out to join her Sapphire Bay friends for brunch, and she hoped it wouldn't be too long before that could happen.

As she waited for the kettle to boil, she realised that Sammy would be fine, and so would she.

'New Year, new start,' she said to the decoration of the bells above the kitchen window. She sat back at the kitchen table, picked up her iPad, and started to scroll for rentals. There weren't many on offer and she wasn't sure that she was ready to commit to a one-year lease on a short-term contract. She wondered if the Beachside Apartments may be available to rent for a couple of terms.

Chapter 24

A feeling of déjà vu settled over Gemma as she turned her car into the driveway of the Beachside Apartments. She was back in unit two, and this time she would be staying for a few months instead of a few weeks.

January had been a whirlwind of job interviews and getting organised. She had been surprised at how quick the process had been. Sammy commented the school must have been desperate for a history teacher!

The contract had been for the first semester, with the possibility of continuing, which meant she would have a job at least until the mid-year school holidays. Instead of getting a rental then possibly having to break the lease if she had to move back to the city, Gemma had decided to rent out an apartment at the Beachside Apartments for the duration and Sammy would stay in the house in the city with some flatmates. Their rent would cover her rent in Sapphire Bay. Gemma would travel back from time to time to do more sorting out in the hope that, if things worked out in Sapphire Bay, she could sell the house at the end of the year, when Sammy had finished her degree, and buy something in Sapphire Bay.

Gemma got her suitcase and pulled it up the stairs. Once again, she abandoned it in the middle of the lounge room and pulled open the blackout curtains. As she opened the glass doors, the air hit her and she stepped outside, taking deep breaths as she did so. She leaned against the railing and took in the view. She had been back less than five minutes and was already feeling better being there.

She pulled out her phone from her pocket and sent Sammy a text message to let her know she had arrived, along with one to Adam. With great reluctance, she turned away and went to finish unpacking the car.

There wasn't much for her to organise, mostly clothes and food from the pantry, along with a few throw rugs and cushions to help her feel more at home. It didn't take her long to get unpacked.

She made a cup of tea and went to stand on the balcony looking over the bay once more.

'Room for one more?' She looked down to see Adam walking up the driveway carrying a package in white butchers paper. He had a backpack slung over one shoulder and she hoped it contained wine. She felt her heart skip a beat at the sight of him and knew she was exactly where she should be.

'Is that fish and chips?' she called down.

'It certainly is,' he replied.

'Then, there's always room,' she laughed and went inside to let him in, putting her glass on the kitchen bench as she passed.

She opened the door and saw him standing there.

'Welcome back to Sapphire Bay,' he said. 'I'm so glad you've returned.'

'Me too,' she said and gave him a huge hug. He wrapped the arm not carrying the food around her and hugged her back. It felt good and she didn't want to let go, but the smell of the fish and chips made her stomach rumble. 'Come on in,' she said as she let go.

***

Later that evening, Gemma and Adam sat on the balcony, sipping wine and talking as the sun went down over the bay.

'Before I forget, Margaret asked me to give you this,' Adam said, reaching into his backpack and handing her a parcel. Gemma unwrapped it and burst into laughter.

'A *World's Greatest Teacher* t-shirt! It's just perfect,' she said between giggles. 'Not sure I'll wear it to school, but I will have to wear it to the library one day to show it off.'

'Margaret is really happy you're back. So are the others. I had to fight them off as they all wanted to come over tonight.' Gemma smiled. It would have been nice to see the gang, but she was happy she had Adam all to herself.

'So am I,' Gemma said. Adam had already told her about the planned brunch on the beach in the morning so she wouldn't be surprised with an early Saturday morning wake up. They sat in comfortable silence for a while.

'Starting on Monday?' Adam said.

'Yep, I'm really looking forward to it,' Gemma replied. 'I'm more excited about starting at Sapphire Bay Secondary than I thought I would be. I thought I'd be nervous and scared.'

'Then it's a sign you're in the right place,' he said and held up his nearly empty glass in a toast. 'To new beginnings.'

'To new beginnings.' She clinked her glass against his. It wasn't only a new job in a new town, but new friendships, and space to see where things may lead.

As they sipped their wine, Gemma felt a sense of calm that she hadn't felt in a long time. She knew she'd come home.

Epilogue – 3 months later

❦

Gemma surprised herself as to how quickly she had settled into a routine in Sapphire Bay. She loved her job at Sapphire Bay Secondary College, there was the usual mix of students from those who were cheeky and disruptive to those who were quiet and studious and everything in between. The staff were a great team to work with, and she still pinched herself at how well things were working out.

She attended trivia most Tuesday nights, and the Pack of Spuds hadn't risen much further in the ranks, but none of them cared. The gang also caught up regularly for paddleboarding and brunch on the beach as well as evenings in the pub, though Gemma still preferred to sit on the beach and watch rather than go in the water. She and Linda would often eat lunch together in the staff room at school, and Gemma quickly came to consider her one of her closest friends.

Of course, there was plenty of time for Gemma and Adam to spend together on their own. They had started work on the book for the 70th anniversary of the Carols by Candlelight and hoped that they would still have a place to hold the celebration in December.

One Saturday morning in late March, Gemma was waiting for him in the café she had eaten her first morning in Sapphire Bay all those months ago. She was pleased to get a table just inside the front window as the wind made it too cold to sit outside.

'I have the most amazing news!' Adam said as he reached the table.

'Oh?' Gemma looked up at him. He had received the cowbell she sent for Christmas, but he never wore it, and still regularly managed to sneak up on her, even when she was watching out for him.

'Late last night, I heard the council have reconsidered. They're redoing the development plans to make sure there's space for the Carols by Candlelight, Foreshore Market, and so many other community events! This delays any works until at least next year, so the Carols can still be on the Foreshore this year.'

'Oh, my goodness,' Gemma stood up and wrapped her arms around him, kissing his cheek without thinking. 'That's wonderful.'

'All your hard work paid off,' he said. 'Going through the archives, the presentation, all of it.'

'All *our* hard work,' she said. He grinned.

'We'd better get the book finished,' he said. She just nodded. They had spent time reaching out to past performers and memories were flowing in, including superstar Abigail Freedman and a couple of the children of Alf and Joan Trevors. They were starting to worry they would have too much material for a single book and would have to produce a whole series!

'Before we sit down,' Gemma said. 'I have some news too.'

'Oh?'

'Yasmine's husband has been offered a job in Perth; they're going to be moving so she won't be returning after her maternity leave. They've offered me her job!'

'That's wonderful,' he said. He pulled her close again, then kissed her on the lips before pulling back in surprise. 'I'm sorry, I...'

'It's okay,' Gemma said quietly. She reached for him and kissed him back. This time the kiss was deliberate.

When they pulled away, they smiled at each other and sat down at the table, pulling their chairs beside each other. As she looked at him, she felt the now familiar calm settle over her.

She was glad she had taken the job back in November. Glad she had trusted herself to make the move in January. Glad she had just kissed this amazing man.

As she looked at him, she couldn't imagine her life being any less perfect than it was in that moment, and for the first time in a long while, she was excited to see what would come next.

Acknowledgements

Writing is a journey, and it's not one I've been able to take on my own. As I write this, I'm a new empty nester, with my children having moved out of home, and I'm beginning a new chapter of my life. Part of that chapter is choosing to do more things that bring me joy — and writing is very much one of them.

I want to thank my good friend and fellow author, **Renee Conoulty**, for her encouragement, for listening to my endless story ideas, and for her thoughtful feedback on this book. Her messages of *"just do it — it doesn't have to be perfect"* arrived exactly when I needed them and helped me find my confidence again.

To **Renita**, a new friend who read early versions of this story and offered support, encouragement, and invaluable feedback — not only on the manuscript, but also on the cover and internal layout. Your generosity, insight, and friendship have meant more to me than I can easily put into words.

To the members of the writers' groups I'm part of, both online and offline: thank you for your support, encouragement, shared wisdom, and stories. Being part of these communities has helped keep me writing, even during times when everything else felt uncertain.

Finally, to my family. I grew up surrounded by stories, and that early love has stayed with me. Your ongoing support and encouragement mean everything. Thank you.

About the author

Melissa Gijsbers is an author and booklover. Stories have always been a big part of her life, and she has been writing them for as long as she can remember. Her first book, *Swallow Me, NOW!*, was published in 2014. At the time of writing this book, she has three picture books, four middle grade books, as well as books of writing prompts published. This is her first novella for grown ups.

She currently lives near Phillip Island in Victoria, Australia and spends quite a bit of time coming up with fun ideas for stories, as well as writing more books herself.

You can find out more about Melissa and her books on her website—www.melissagijsbers.com

www.ingramcontent.com/pod-product-compliance
Lightning Source LLC
Chambersburg PA
CBHW070448170726
48291CB00005B/1660